DREAMWEAVER

"Troy Morrison! Report at once to the Exodus flight lounge! Boarding is due to commence in ten minutes!"

Hastily Troy turned to re-enter the corridor – and the girl was standing behind him. She was little more than a child, maybe eight or nine years old, with long dark hair and tangerine-coloured eyes. It was her eyes that held him, shining orange, brilliant eyes gazing into his and seeing him as clearly as he saw her. She was not from Earth, he thought. No ethnic group had eyes that colour. He opened his mouth to speak to her, to ask who she was and where she came from, but suddenly she vanished into thin air and was gone.

The girl with tangerine-coloured eyes was an alien.

by the same author

The Llandor Trilogy
Journey Through Llandor
The Road to Irriyan
The Shadow of Mordican

Children of the Dust
Moonwind
Warriors of Taan

DREAMWEAVER

LOUISE LAWRENCE

Collins
An imprint of HarperCollinsPublishers

First published in Great Britain by Collins 1996
This paperback edition published 1997

1 3 5 7 9 10 8 6 4 2

Collins is an imprint of HarperCollins*Publishers* Ltd,
77-85 Fulham Palace Road, Hammersmith, London W6 8JB.

ISBN 0 00 675088-5

Set in R Stempel Garamond
Printed and bound in Great Britain by
Caledonian International Book Manufacturing Ltd, Glasgow, G64

To my husband, Graham

CHAPTER ONE

"All passengers and relevant personnel report to the Exodus flight lounge," a tinny voice announced. "Boarding is due to begin in thirty minutes."

"That's us," said Mrs Guttenham.

"We'd better go," said Hannah.

"There's no hurry," Mr Guttenham replied.

"They can wait for us anyway," Ivan said arrogantly.

Troy Morrison also paid no heed to the announcement. Leaning on the railing of the observation platform he gazed upon the planet the Guttenhams had come from but where he had never been. Cloud formations drifted in swirls of white. Oceans shimmered turquoise in the sunlight, foamed against rocky headlands or creamed along sandy shores. Southwards, he could see the outline of the Americas – a patch of green preserved darkness that marked the Amazon basin, the Mexican isthmus and the bleached prairies of the mid-west states. Northwards were the five great lakes, the Canadian pine forests and the tundra already whitened by approaching winter.

Troy had gazed upon Earth before, many thousands of times during his seventeen years in the space-station that wheeled above it. Its perfection invariably stunned him. Among the black and gold of surrounding space its colours glowed like a great blue jewel. But the reality was different. Daily television reports and scientific observation painted a sadder picture. The Earth was dying. Patches of poisonous algae stained the polluted seas. Acid rain poisoned the lakes and rivers. Local wars laid the land to waste. Cities decayed and forests were felled. Deserts and dust-bowls spread and crops failed to thrive. There was disease there, and famine, and whole populations sickened and starved.

What had happened on Earth made him angry. A whole vast world, and they had despoiled it. Troy recalled its history from an education tape, a succession of civilisations built on serfdom and slavery that rose and fell. The human race never seemed to learn, his tutor had remarked. Wherever they went in the galaxy, they made the same mistakes – except on board the orbiting space-stations. There, the regimented routine and the conditions of cramped co-existence made Troy ultra-sensitive to impositions that eroded his own or anyone else's freedom.

"All passengers and relevant personnel report to the Exodus flight lounge," the tinny voice repeated. "Boarding is due to begin in twenty-five minutes."

"We ought to go," Hannah said again.

"I wish we didn't have to," murmured her mother.

"This is no time to have doubts," said Mr Guttenham.

"There's nothing left for us on Earth anyway," said Ivan.

"Only our friends," retorted Hannah.

"Acquaintances, my dear," said Mr Guttenham.

"And the Kirkengards are coming with us," said Ivan.

Troy glanced at them, a wealthy American family – father, mother and two teenage offspring – typical of the passenger list he had studied. People like the Guttenhams, who had money enough to pay for a seat on the shuttle and a cryogenic berth aboard a spaceship, were leaving Earth in droves. Japanese company directors, British arms dealers, Syrian mercenaries and Korean manufacturers, American police chiefs and attorneys, Arab sheikhs and international television stars – anyone who was someone studied the virtual reality videos compiled from the reports of the survey ships and headed for another planet. The four biospheric space-stations, set up as an experiment midway through the twenty-first century to provide a solution for the population overspill, now had a different purpose – emigration staging posts between Earth and the stars.

As each ship left another was built, a whole fleet fanning outwards across the galaxy seeking suitable worlds on which to settle. It was an old tradition, human and heroic, the true pioneering spirit. Elsewhere, as they had once done in America, colonists set up their communities, tamed the wilderness and began a new civilisation. And on *Exodus 27*, along with the Guttenhams and three thousand others, Troy would go – to a planetary system revolving round Croxley's Star.

Survey ships, charting the galaxy, were not built to land and take off again. The surveying of each Earth-type planet was done from orbit. Various scanning techniques ascertained the climatic conditions and geological structure, and tiny robotic landing craft were sent to the surface to collect samples of soil and water and scraps of vegetation that were tested in sterile laboratories for viruses, bacteria and toxins. From countless scientific studies, and enlarged aerial photographs showing flora and fauna, population distribution and possible landing sites, each virtual reality video was built up. The video for the planet that revolved round Croxley's Star showed a world that was green and brown, beautiful and beguiling. And there Troy would carve out a future for himself.

"Will all passengers and relevant personnel report to the Exodus flight lounge," the announcer repeated yet again. "Boarding is due to begin in twenty minutes."

"I shall miss it," mourned Mrs Guttenham.

"It was such a nice house," said Hannah.

"It was for ever being burgled," said Ivan.

"And we shall have a palace where we are going," said Mr Guttenham. "A palace, my dear, and a million-acre spread."

"Guttenhamland," said Ivan.

The dreams of most emigrants were similar, but Troy's were different. He just wanted to get away from the space-station, to escape from the vast enclosed biosphere that was sterile and seasonless, the recycled air and water. He wanted to stand on solid ground beneath an open sky, feel the sun on his face and the wind in his hair, the wetness of rain and the coolness of shadows. He wanted to be

11

unconfined and walk where he would, released from the walls and ceilings, the long curving corridors and cubby-hole rooms that imprisoned him, free to explore the landscape of another world, live in an environment where everything was not already known and classified and discovered. Mysteriousness drew him and for the first time in his life he felt a thrill of excitement.

"It all looked so primitive," Mrs Guttenham complained.

"No domestic robots or modern conveniences," said Hannah.

"No shops," said Mrs Guttenham.

"Give us a few years," said Mr Guttenham.

"We're simply not used to roughing it," said Mrs Guttenham.

"We'll have servants, my dear."

"The pick of the native labour force," said Ivan.

It was an assumption that triggered Troy's anger. What gave Ivan Guttenham or anyone else the right to make slaves of people? Yet most planets chosen for colonisation had native populations, and the planet *Exodus 27* was scheduled to land on was no exception. And the indigenous people there would have little choice but to co-operate. Civilisation was heading their way whether they wanted it or not, and servitude and hard labour was their likely fate.

Thinking about it, Troy felt increasingly uneasy. He wanted to warn them, scream across the universe through seven light years of space and time.

"I'll be grey-haired when we arrive," said Mrs Guttenham.

"And I'll be twenty-four," said Hannah.

Troy could have reassured them. Biological ageing was suspended by the cryogenic process. He, too, would be twenty-four – yet hardly a day older than he was now. Travelling faster than the speed of light on board *Exodus 27*, age and time would become irrelevant. The seven years the journey was estimated to take would pass and he would know nothing about it. Apart from the six months of monitoring duty he was scheduled to make, he would be sealed in a cryogenic chamber, his life functions suspended, his breathing and heartbeats barely perceptible – seven undreaming years of theta sleep until the ship slowed and entered its final orbit. And then...

"Will Troy Morrison report to the flight departure lounge!" announced the voice from the tannoy system. "Troy Morrison to the flight departure lounge, please."

Automatically, Troy responded, straightened the lapels of his silver uniform and pulled down the cuffs in readiness.

"He's one of the crew!" hissed Hannah.

He was indeed, trained and qualified, a junior bio-technician assigned to their flight, his mother a senior Flight Officer transferred from the shuttle service, his father a computer programmer aboard the space-station and similarly transferred. With one last glance at Earth, and pointedly ignoring the Guttenhams, Troy left the observation platform. Harsh light dazzled him from the ceiling high above his head and a great curving corridor led him round the rim of the space-station.

It was built like a wheel. Living quarters, laboratories and workshops were housed at various levels around the rim. And the spokes contained the fish farms and agricultural units, the recycling unit and protein processing plants. Arches and doorways made of plasti-glass opened onto inner spaces huge as fifty cathedrals, allowing vistas of green hydroponic jungles as Troy passed by.

Would it be similar? he wondered. The unnamed world to which he was going? He had seen it on the computer screen but he could not imagine it – the rank smell of the open air, equatorial forests or deciduous woodlands, the sensation of mountains or prairies and the uncaged creatures that lived there. The true reality was beyond his experience. And when the ship arrived the planet would change anyway. The dreams of Mr Guttenham would be speedily imposed and the colonists would carve up the land between them. They would begin again what the human race had almost completed on Earth, the civilising process of planetary destruction. And Troy would be unavoidably a part of that process, because he was there.

Again he felt the urge to warn the native people who lived on the planet. Stepping onto another observation platform, he gripped the railing and gazed at the stars through the plasti-glass barrier. His voice would not reach light years across the galaxy, but maybe his thoughts would. He sent them spinning outwards.

"Are you listening? Are you receiving me? You've got seven years left in which to do something!"

But only the tannoy system answered him, and this time it was his mother speaking – J. Verity Morrison, a senior Flight Officer, her voice clipped and efficient.

"Troy Morrison? Report at once to the Exodus flight lounge! Boarding is due to commence in ten minutes and you were sent to fetch the ram-card key for the main computer. So where is it?"

Hastily, forgetting all else, Troy turned to re-enter the corridor. And the girl was standing behind him: a dusky-skinned child, maybe eight or nine years old, with long dark hair and tangerine eyes. There were multi-coloured bangles on her arms, a pale yellow crystal strung on a leather thong across her brow, and she wore a simple white shift fashioned from some linen-type fabric. But it was her eyes that held him, shining orange, brilliant eyes gazing into his and seeing him as clearly as he saw her. His heartbeat quickened. She was not from Earth, he thought. No ethnic group had eyes that colour. He opened his mouth to speak to her, to ask who she was and where she came from, but suddenly she vanished into thin air and was gone.

Troy stared in bewilderment, then frowned and began to reason. It must have been a holographic image he had seen, although he could have sworn the child was really there, that her eyes had perceived just as his eyes did and she had been aware of both him and her surroundings. And what hi-tech culture had developed the hologram to that degree of perfection? And who had beamed her image aboard the space-station? No one on Earth, he decided, because the girl with tangerine eyes had been alien.

His mother's voice disturbed his thoughts, threatened him across the tannoy system. "Troy Morrison? If that ram-key fails to reach us within the next sixty seconds you can forget about your boarding pass! You'll be facing the space-station disciplinary committee and recycling faeces for the

16

next seven years of your life!"

Troy heard and remembered space-station rules. Anything untoward, any hint of alien activity, any suspicion of an intelligence elsewhere in the universe that might be more advanced than their own, required an immediate red alert. And, as there was no way he could reach the flight lounge within the allotted sixty seconds, he needed to instigate a diversion. And the Guttenhams, strolling in a leisurely way towards him along the corridor, must surely have seen what he had seen and would back him up. Unhesitatingly, Troy pressed the alarm button, delaying their departure, their pursuit of happiness and all their dreams.

CHAPTER TWO

Eth discarded her night-shift, dressed in her day clothes, replaced the bangles on her arms and carefully tucked the yellow crystal beneath her pillow. Nemony had loaned it to soothe her nightmares but she had dreamed anyway – a strange dream, she told her mother.

Standing before the window in the main room of the house, she saw Malroth low on the horizon, a burnished red world sinking towards the western mountains, its desert sands reflecting the dawn of the Roth Star. Staring at it, Eth could make out the shadows of its ridges, the dark scars of its valleys, the shine of the great river delta that drained into an ocean of marsh, a hint of green across the distance. It was definitely not Malroth she had seen in her dream, nor Arbroth either, the planet on which she lived. Arbroth was oceanless, a world of forests, lakes and mountains. The world she had gazed upon had been a world of water, where continents lay like islands and the surrounding seas shone blue as the summer sky. And the companion world revolving round it had been dusty and lifeless, white as bleached bone.

"I went towards the blue world," said Eth. "It was as if I was drawn towards it by an invisible thread."

Kanderin, her mother, braided the tresses of her hair.

"What happened then?" she asked.

"There was a wheel," said Eth, "spinning above it, made of silvery metal with spokes of glass. Huge it was, and lit from within, and there were many windows round the rim. What drew me was actually inside it."

"What a stupid dream," said Arlynn.

Eth turned her head. "I haven't finished yet!"

"Go on," said Kanderin. "And do stand still."

"Something seemed to pull me in through its walls," said Eth. "There was a long curved corridor and an odd-looking boy was standing there. He was older than Liadd…"

"Don't bring me into it!" her brother said roughly.

"I'm not!" said Eth. "All I said was—"

19

"Just get on with it!" said Arlynn.

"He wasn't like us at all," said Eth. "His skin was pale as the under-belly of a slime-crawler and his hair was the colour of ripe grain. He wore a tight silver suit and his eyes were blue."

"Blue eyes?" said Arlynn. "How can anyone have blue eyes, Eth?"

"I told you he was odd," said Eth.

"Were you frightened of him?" asked Kanderin.

"No," said Eth. "I wasn't frightened at all."

"So what happened next?" asked Arlynn.

"I think he wanted to tell me something," said Eth. "But he didn't have time. You woke me up instead."

With a last tug at her hair her mother released her to join the others at the breakfast table. There were slabs of coarse bread, a dish of curd cheese, beakers of shote's milk and garrameal porridge that steamed in a painted tureen. Shafts of light from the Roth Star shone on the white-washed walls and glowed in the woven colours of the carpet that covered the floor. Outside, in the early morning, the village stirred. A barn fowl crowed. Zuke, the carpenter, opened the shutters of his workshop on the opposite side of the street and shoteherders drove their shaggy flocks towards the high pastures.

"What a stupid dream!" Arlynn said again.

"It was better than yours!" retorted Eth.

"Mine had meaning," said Arlynn.

"The marrying fair," scoffed Liadd.

"What's wrong with that?" Arlynn said sharply.

Liadd smiled smugly. "There's no room for a husband in this house," he said, "not with me here. And it's another five years before I reach the age of majority and mother has the right to turn me out."

Kanderin's voice reproved him gently. "Why should I want to turn you out, Liadd?"

"You turned my father out!" he said angrily.

"He left!" Arlynn said hotly.

"And why was that?" retorted Liadd.

Eth did not know why her father had left but sometimes Liadd reminded her of him, especially when he was angry as he was now. Now she could look at him and remember that other face: glowering, bearded, distorted with rage. She could remember the weals on her buttocks, the blood from Arlynn's split lip and blue–black bruises on her mother's skin. It was all Aldo was to Eth – great hurting hands, a too-loud voice, a terrifying inescapable presence, filling her early years with fear and pain and tears – until one morning she had awoken and found him gone. Since then, other men had been her father, good, kind men, men of the village, caring for her and her mother, Liadd and Arlynn.

"I know what they say!" Liadd went on.

"Who?" asked Kanderin,

"Everyone!" said Liadd. "You had that woman cast him out!"

"What woman?" asked Eth.

"He means Nemony," said Arlynn.

"The dreamweaver!" Liadd said harshly.

Eth added honey and spooned up her porridge. Every village had its dreamweaver and she liked Nemony. She was tall and graceful and her orange eyes glowed with a magical light, and her smile was bright and her voice was gentle. She lived in a small stone cottage beyond the village, alone, except for Brenner who was her acolyte, Brenner the simpleton who slept on a bench by the fire and helped her do the chores. Nemony grew herbs and brewed potions, visited people in their homes in times of trouble. She could interpret dreams and cure nightmares and had loaned Eth the sleep crystal. Zuke called her a witch and some of the village men were uneasy in her company. But she was a member of the village council and would not do anything ill, thought Eth. And Aldo had been big and strong, a brute of a man most women said, so how could Nemony have cast him out?

"She couldn't possibly," said Eth.

Liadd turned on her. His eyes were hard and his voice was scathing. "What do you know about it?

You're just a dim-brained girl and I don't need your opinion! So keep your big mouth out of it!"

Tears prickled Eth's eyes. Sometimes Liadd was horrible.

"Don't speak to your sister like that," Kanderin chided.

"She's done nothing to you," said Arlynn.

"That's right!" snarled Liadd. "Stick up for her! All women together! Keep the menfolk in their places! I'm beginning to know what my father went through! And I'm not surprised he lashed out!" He picked up the bread knife. "You three make me want to vomit!" he said.

He slammed it down, its blade piercing the table top. Then he was gone, banging the door behind him, heading up the cobbled street to the schoolroom, kicking a stone and calling loudly to Zuke's two sons as he went.

"What's wrong with him?" Eth asked tearfully.

"He takes after his father!" Arlynn said angrily.

"It's probably his age," Kanderin sighed.

"Puberty," said Arlynn. "And that's no excuse!"

"What's puberty?" asked Eth.

"Growing up!" Arlynn said curtly.

"The phase between boyhood and manhood," Kanderin murmured. "It's a difficult time for him, Arlynn."

"Not just for him!" Arlynn said huffily. "And what if it goes on? Can we really live with this kind of behaviour for another five years?"

Kanderin made no answer. Her orange eyes were troubled. Frown-lines creased her brow and her work-roughened hands reached for the dish of curd cheese and found it empty. Liadd had eaten it all with no thought for anyone but himself. Kanderin sighed again, went to the pantry and returned with a pot of burlberry jam.

"He'll be apprenticed to Yordan soon," she said. "Work will calm him."

"What if it doesn't?" Arlynn asked.

"Then I will have failed in my upbringing," Kanderin declared.

Arlynn shook her head. "It's in his blood, Mother, and now it's coming out, and that is no reflection on you. Speak to Nemony about him, please, for all our sakes."

The knife stayed upright in the table and Kanderin stared at it.

"It's just a passing phase," she insisted. "And it's too soon to call attention to him, Arlynn, or admit he is a problem. I'd rather not consult Nemony yet."

Along the street the school bell rang, summoning Eth to lessons. When the day's schooling was finished she would go and ask Nemony about the

24

new word, puberty, she decided, and tell her the details of her dream.

The woods smelled of earth and the coming autumn, rich with nuts and fungi and a few coloured leaves beginning to fall. Eth scuffed through them, their dry rustling sounds drowning the voices of children who played at the lakeside.

It was late afternoon, the mountains above her turning blue with shadows and the Roth Star sinking towards the peak of the Edderhorn, when she reached Nemony's cottage. It stood at the end of the track between forest and meadows and mountains, its front door closed, its windows reflecting the light. Eth opened the gate to the walled garden and headed up the path, her steps releasing a scent of crushed herbs – woundwort and shote's bane, blue–black painsease and the heart-shaped leaves of lovegloss. Their tangy perfumes mingled with a smell of woodsmoke from the cottage chimney and fallen tartfruit rotting beneath a tree. Dozens of tiny minces with twitching whiskers, and a crowd of whiteflies, fed on the sour fermenting juices.

"Nemony!" called Eth.

Only the silence answered. Disappointed, Eth turned to leave, but Brenner came from the back of the cottage with his arms full of split logs. He stacked them by the doorway and grinned at Eth, an inane grin showing rotting teeth and a huge mis-shapen tongue. His pale orange eyes watered in the sunlight and he struggled to tell her, struggled to formulate the words.

"N-Nemony...gone...v-village."

"Will she be back soon?" asked Eth.

"Sh-she with Olna, b-birthing...Yordan's...wife."

"Oh," said Eth.

"You w-want...to wait?"

"No," said Eth. "Babies can take all night sometimes. Tell her I'll call again tomorrow."

Brenner nodded and Eth headed home again. And where the track became a cobbled side lane leading past the schoolroom to the village square, she met Nemony. The birthing was over. Blood stained Nemony's dress. Pallor and sadness marked her face. It was a boy born dead, she said. Yordan was no father after all, and Zella no mother. And twice that day Eth had been touched by adult pain and adult experiences she did not understand.

"Have you been to see me?" asked Nemony.

"I had a dream," said Eth.

"Another nightmare?" asked Nemony.

"No," said Eth. "It was just a dream and it doesn't matter."

"Dreams always matter," Nemony said.

"Remember it and come and tell me tomorrow."

Eth nodded and went on her way, past the Council Hall, and the trans-matt terminal in the village square. It was a smooth black pyramid that would open to reveal a glass sarcophagus in which the dead baby's body would be placed. Eth remembered other death days: the people gathered in the square, the hum of light from within the terminal and the slow closing of the lid. It was automatic: pre-set co-ordinates transferred the corpse to its cremation in the fires of Arbroth. And into the trans-matt terminal Eth herself would be placed, one day, when her body died and her present life ended.

She gazed at it fearfully. She had nightmares about it, a trans-matt terminal much bigger than this one and herself stepping into it alive. And that night she dreamt of it again – a huge trans-matt terminal full of glass sarcophagi. But the destination of its corpses was ice, not fire, and she was not its victim. Stars moved beyond the window as the boy closed his eyes and died.

CHAPTER THREE

The moon slid past the window, pock-marked and pale, as *Exodus 27* headed outwards into the solar system. The switch to warp speed was not due for several days yet but Troy would in any case not see it. He was already dressed in a white sleep-suit and would go to his cryogenic berth at the end of the present shift. And after the hassle he had caused at the space-station, there was no appeal. A full-scale search had found no trace of an alien presence, no evidence that the girl he claimed he had seen had ever been there. She was dismissed as a hallucination, a symptom of space-sickness, and Troy's mental and emotional stability were consequently suspect. Out of all the crew he was the most expendable. No responsible Flight Officer, let alone his mother, would willingly extend his period on duty, and his six months on the "awake" schedule were up for question as well. He shivered and glanced at his wrist watch. Luminous digits told him he had one hour left to enjoy the sensation of consciousness.

"Feeling nervous?" Dr Wynn-Stanley inquired.

"Not particularly," said Troy.

"Many people do," the medic informed him. "When it comes to the crunch they see it as seven years of death and I have to sedate them."

Troy shrugged. "The sooner I sleep the sooner I get where we're going," he said. "So what's the point in staying awake?"

"That's a fair rationale," said Dr Wynn-Stanley.

Less than four hours into its flight, except for the bridge and the crew quarters, the main bulk of the ship was already shutting down. Its cargo hatches were sealed. The lights had dimmed in its cavernous cryogenic chambers and the surrounding air was turning icy. Accompanying Dr Wynn-Stanley on the bio-check rounds, Troy shivered again. Whoever took over from him would need to wear a thermal suit.

His weighted boots clattered over the air-conditioning grids and the ship's computers churred softly in the background. Data panels at the foot of each plasti-glass berth glowed eerily blue. It was like walking through a crypt full of transparent coffins, gazing in turn at the incumbent dead – except that they were not dead but sleeping. Electrode helmets monitored their brainwaves and pulse rates. Iron lungs breathed for them once every four minutes. Controlled by the computer, their life functions were slowed and their dreams suspended. The blue glowing panels, which provided a current read-out of every individual's biological status, would be regularly checked by on-duty staff throughout the seven years of flight, and would flash to red and raise an automatic alarm if the cryogenics malfunctioned or the life signs faltered and failed.

According to Dr Wynn-Stanley it seldom happened. Systems on board the Exodus fleet did not break down and all passengers underwent rigorous medical tests before being accepted for emigration. But very occasionally something was missed: the thinning of an artery that could lead to aneurysm, a thrombosis that could trigger a stroke or a heart-attack, or a rare progressive disease missed at the onset that might prove fatal.

"Hence the need for regular checks," the doctor explained.

Troy nodded.

That was Jack Wynn-Stanley's job but his, as a bio-technician, was different. He had to check the wires and filaments, the cryogenic berths themselves and all that connected them to the ship's computer system. The blue lights simply told him that technically all was well. It was down to the medic to interpret the physical information on the data panels: the undulating patterns of brainwaves and heartbeats, blood pressure readings, oxygen levels, white cell counts, and whatever else. Nevertheless, when confronted by the Guttenham family lying side by side in their freezing sleep, Troy could not remain totally impersonal.

"Idiots!" he said.

"Friends of yours?" asked Dr Wynn-Stanley.

"You were present at the inquiry," said Troy.

"Ah," said the doctor. "So this was the family."

"The Guttenhams," said Troy. "I nearly got grounded thanks to them! They were right there, in the corridor, and they must have seen her!"

"The dusky-skinned maiden, you mean?"

"She was a child," said Troy. "And they said they saw no one! Hallucination my foot! It was their testimony that caused that conclusion. And it goes on my record – flaming space-sickness! After seventeen years in orbit! I ask you – is that really likely? I was born in space, for Christ's sake! And the girl I saw was real!"

Troy's breath smoked in the chill air, and frost patterns had formed on the plasti-glass surface above Hannah Guttenham's face. Dr Wynn-Stanley bent to read the bio-data.

"If it's any consolation I voted to accept your account."

"I appreciate that," Troy said stiffly.

"I believe you did see what you saw."

"Then why didn't my mother—?"

"Because it was their word against yours, Troy, and the word of a merchant banker carries more weight. And what if you had been believed? An alien intruder aboard the space-station is a serious matter. We'd have spent the next nine months on red alert and the flight would have been aborted."

"Suppose it happens again?" said Troy.

"If it does," said the medic, "you won't be aware of it. You'll be deep in theta sleep. It may provide a problem for whichever Flight Officer happens to be on duty but not for you – unless it's a phenomenon confined to the space-station, of course. Either way I'd advise you to forget about it."

"I already have," Troy lied.

Jack Wynn-Stanley smiled and patted his shoulder, bent before Ivan Guttenham's berth and checked the readings, then moved on to the next man. Fritz Johann Guttenham, the data panel read. Germano-

American. Date of birth 099/6/22. Blood group O.

"The founding father-to-be of Guttenhamland," Troy announced.

The medic glanced at him. "You don't approve of that?"

"Meaning you do?" asked Troy.

"I'm from Earth," Dr Wynn-Stanley reminded him. "There it's a common enough aspiration. We all want to be kings of our own kingdom."

"It's the native people I'm thinking of," said Troy.

"There are acreage restrictions and various other guidelines."

"With no one to enforce them," Troy said bitterly.

Jack Wynn-Stanley sighed and straightened his back. "Don't assume personal responsibility for the whole universe, Troy. Leave that to God."

"After Christ there were never any signs of divine intervention on Earth," said Troy. "According to the history tapes I studied, God did nothing to save the way of life of the Sioux or the pigmy or the Australian aborigine, so why should He put Himself out for the people of Croxley's Star?"

"And what can you do about it?" Dr Wynn-Stanley asked him. "Apart from sabotaging the ship and murdering its occupants?"

"Nothing," said Troy.

"Then I'd advise you to forget about that, too."

33

The metal railings were slick with ice beneath Troy's fingers and his boots rattled on the gantry as he and the medic climbed to inspect the upper tiers of cryogenic berths. Blue light reflected on the older man's spectacles as he bent to continue his task. But Troy could not forget.

"I wanted to warn them," he said. "And that's when I saw her."

"You think there's a connection?" asked the medic.

"Not necessarily," Troy said cagily.

"Yet you felt the need to mention it," said Dr Wynn-Stanley. "Why is that, I wonder? Telepathic contact across half the length of the galaxy is hardly a believable hypothesis. Could she, perhaps, have been a mental projection born of your own emotional desire?"

"I thought you were on my side!" said Troy.

"I am," said the medic. "I merely question your theorising, that's all. It's unscientific, Troy, but I'll make a note of it. And do you want me to inform your mother?"

"She wouldn't want to know anyway," Troy said huffily.

The medic grinned.

"No emotional goodbyes between you and Verity then? Just as well, perhaps – seven years is a long separation. But let's hope the eventual reunion will be less abrasive, shall we? In you go."

"Pardon?" said Troy.

"This is where we part company," Dr Wynn-Stanley said. "Troy Morrison – that's you, isn't it? And right by the window, too."

Troy stared at the open berth, and an unadmitted fear tightened the nerves of his stomach. "Don't I even get a last meal?" he said.

"That would ruin the effects of the enema," replied the medic.

"I'll just check the computer link," said Troy.

His hands shook when he loosened the coupling socket. The red light flashed its warning and changed to blue when he tightened it again. He nodded, satisfied with its functioning, but the fear remained. He had to get a grip on himself, tell himself silently several times that it was not death he was facing but seven years of sleep. Then he stepped inside the cryogenic berth. Its soft contours moulded to his body and the electrode helmet lowered to grip his skull.

"Pulse rapid, blood pressure rising," read Dr Wynn-Stanley. "You're hyper-ventilating, too. I thought you said it didn't worry you?"

"You wait till it's your turn," Troy muttered.

"Do you want me to give you a shot?"

"No," said Troy.

"Then I'll see you tomorrow," the medic said.

"Seven years from now," said Troy.

"Four years," corrected Dr Wynn-Stanley. "We're on the 'awake' shift together, remember?"

"My 'awake' shift is likely to be cancelled," muttered Troy.

"If it is," said the medic, "I'll see you in orbit."

"I'd rather that anyway," said Troy. "Who wants to go through this twice?"

"Changed your mind about the shot?"

"No," said Troy.

Jack Wynn-Stanley nodded and closed the plasti-glass door. It sealed with a hermetic sigh and the pre-cryogenics switched themselves on. It was warmth Troy felt, and soft therapeutic music calmed his fear. The inspection panel beyond his feet filled the berth with quiet blue light, sleep-inducing, all of it, although how long he took to succumb was up to him. The freezing process would not begin until his brainwaves slowed and dipped into a natural theta rhythm.

Outside the plasti-glass berth the medic remained, checked Troy's bio-readings, raised his thumb in a gesture of satisfaction and soundlessly departed. In the vast spaces of the cryogenic chamber, among three thousand other sleepers, Troy was alone with the warmth and the music and the soft blue light.

Stars slid slowly past the porthole window and he had all the time he needed to meditate on things – until he slept. Then, when he awoke, he would be in the vicinity of Croxley's Star – in orbit, perhaps, around the unnamed world on which the ship would eventually land – a planet of lakes and forests and mountains, green and unspoiled, until Mr Guttenham arrived.

Troy's fists clenched. It should not be allowed to happen, he thought. That world belonged to its native population, not to Mr Guttenham or anyone else on board this ship. They had no right to take it for themselves, no right to impose their own ideas of civilisation on a primitive society. Renewed anger triggered a surge of adrenalin and his heartbeat speeded up, but there was no one around to notice it... or was there?

Through the mist made on the plasti-glass by the ducted warmth and Troy's own breath, a pair of orange eyes gazed into his.

The child had returned. Dim light sparkled on the lemon-coloured crystal she wore on her forehead, made a blue sheen on the dark, tousled tresses of her hair. A small dusky apparition, she stood outside on the gantry and stared at him. And he, confined in his transparent coffin, could neither move nor speak to her, however much he wanted to. In the soundproofed booth his words would not reach her and he could not set himself free.

Troy closed his eyes in a moment of frustration and, when he opened them again, the girl was gone. For a while her image haunted him but soon he would cease to remember her, or think or dream. She would age as he slept and grow towards womanhood...and light years would pass before Troy was to see her again.

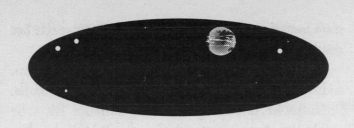

CHAPTER FOUR

"It was a huge trans-matt terminal," sobbed Eth. "I was inside it and so was he. He closed his eyes and died. And then I woke up."

Apple logs sizzled on the fire. Nemony leaned forward and gripped Eth's hands. "Listen," she said. "I've explained to you before about the trans-matt system. It's a way of transporting people from place to place but they don't have to be dead."

"They are in our village," sobbed Eth.

"That's because it's a small old-fashioned terminal with a one-way setting," said Nemony. "It will be replaced soon. Then everyone will be able to travel."

"But I know he was dead," wept Eth. "They were all dead. Hundreds and hundreds of people in their glass sarcophagi with frost on their faces – frozen dead, Nemony – and he among them."

"It was only a dream," Nemony said soothingly.

Eth wiped away her tears on the hem of her kirtle.

"But what does it mean?" she asked.

The dreamweaver frowned and shook her head.

"I really don't know," she said. "I'll ask Mistress Agla, she's due to visit us any day now. Meanwhile put it from your mind, Eth, and forget it."

Weeks passed but Eth did not forget. And when the leaves had fallen from the forest trees and early frosts made patterns on the windows at night, the dreamweaver sent word to the school requesting her presence. She was to tell her dreams again, but this time not just to Nemony.

An old woman sat in the inglenook, warming her bones by the fire. Her face was lined with age, dry as parchment and browned by the weather. She had a hawk-nose and bright fierce eyes and her hair, plaited tightly in a single braid, was peppered with grey. Her black gown was stained by travel. And a grey-robed acolyte sat beside her, clutching a tankard of mulled ale, his face hidden by his hood.

Eth paid little heed to him. It was Mistress Agla who held her attention, an adjudicator from the Dreamweavers' Guild making an unscheduled visit. Usually she came but once a year, between hay time and harvest, arriving in the evening when Malroth cast its blood-red light on the village street. But now she had returned unexpectedly... the misty rain and the racket in the schoolroom concealing the clatter of the jendo's hooves on the cobbles as she passed outside. And although Eth had seen fresh piles of droppings on the forest track, she had thought nothing of it. Not until Nemony opened the door to her knock did she realise who was there.

Now the fierce eyes frightened her. Village rumours and the old woman's power made her want to run. But a crooked finger beckoned and her smile seemed friendly. "Come here, child. Come and sit on this stool by me. I want you to tell me of these dreams of yours."

Nervously, Eth regarded her.

"Go on," urged Nemony.

"Vashlian and I have come a long way to meet you," said Mistress Agla. "You will not disappoint us, will you?"

"And I have baked honey buns," Nemony said persuasively.

Eth stayed, sat on the stool by the fire, nibbling buns and sipping herb tea. Her voice, shy at first, grew steadily more bold. She told of the great wheel spinning around a turquoise world and the boy she had seen there. And she told the other dream, too, about a great hall full of dim blue light containing hundreds of frozen people and the same boy shut alive in a trans-matt terminal, his blue eyes closing in death.

"When I woke up, I cried," said Eth. "As if it were real."

"Maybe it was," Mistress Agla said matter-of-factly.

"Can that be possible?" asked Nemony.

"Possible indeed," the old woman replied.

"So you think Eth was dream-walking? And it was not a dream at all? But she's so young, Mistress Agla, to have an out-of-body experience."

"I have known stranger things happen in my lifetime to girls younger than this one," said Mistress Agla.

"But what does it mean?" asked Nemony.

Vashlian, the robed acolyte, turned his head. His hard orange stare fixed on Eth's face. He studied her intently. "With your permission...?" he murmured.

"Of course," Mistress Agla replied.

In a low voice the acolyte began to question Eth.

"Tell me more about your second dream, girl. Were the people you saw in their sarcophagi within the wheel you told us of in the first dream? Or were they elsewhere? Describe your surroundings for me."

Eth pondered for a moment.

"I only saw the dim blue light and metal walls, and stars beyond a little round window moving slowly past."

"Moving?" said Vashlian. "Are you sure of that?"

"Yes," said Eth.

"And are you also sure those people were dead?"

"Frozen dead," Eth said sadly. "There was frost on the glass above their faces."

"Humidity," Vashlian murmured. "And that suggests they were still breathing." He turned to Mistress Agla. "You did well to contact me, old woman."

"So what does it mean?" Nemony repeated.

The acolyte frowned.

"I could hazard a guess," he said quietly. "It is not generally known, but some years ago there were reports of a strange metallic star revolving around Arbroth and small machines landing in various places on the planet's surface. They came from the metallic star, it was said, and likewise returned there until the star itself receded into the universe and vanished from our sight."

"And you think there is a connection?" asked Mistress Agla.

"Unless you would have me believe in coincidence," Vashlian said. "Keep me informed if the child has further similar experiences, old woman."

Mistress Agla regarded him. "It is important, Vashlian?"

"It could be vitally important," the acolyte replied.

"In that case…" Mistress Agla turned her gaze on Eth. "What did Nemony say your name was, child?"

"It's Eth," said Nemony.

"Eth," the old woman repeated.

Eth could barely understand what they talked of but the old woman's eyes stayed fixed on her, bright and piercing, seeming to read the truth that was inside her and all the wrong things she had ever done. Her mother's words echoed angrily in her mind. "The adjudicator will know if you misbehave! You wait until she comes!" Eth hung her head. For three days in the year Mistress Agla sat in the judgement seat in the village Council Hall and who knew whether the next time Eth's name might not be mentioned? But the aged voice was gentle when she spoke.

"You've no need to fear me, child. The power I possess can be yours, too, one day. How would you like to have Nemony teach you and become a dreamweaver yourself?"

"Eth's not even pubescent yet," Nemony objected.

"I am aware of that," Mistress Agla retorted.

"She's far too young to make that kind of decision."

"Should she prove to be unsuited…"

"Would it not be better to wait a few more years?"

Vashlian leaned forward. "We may not have a few more years," he said curtly. "If these dreams of hers are real, and if they are linked to those former events, then think what they may portend. She has seen an army frozen in transit, pale-skinned warriors from the stars! And they could be heading here to Arbroth! If we are a target for attack, we need to know, Mistress, and maybe none but this child can tell us!"

Mistress Agla nodded. "Vashlian speaks true, Nemony. We cannot wait for Eth's growing. You must begin teaching her now, my dear. Teach her to control her dream-walking and teach her to dreamweave, too. We must have her functioning as soon as possible."

Nemony frowned, and her lips tightened obstinately.

"Firstly she has to be willing, Mistress Agla. And secondly we will require her mother's permission."

The old woman raised a questioning eyebrow.

"Will the woman withhold it?" she asked. "To count one's daughter a member of the Dreamweavers' Guild is every woman's hope. And of course the child is willing. Is that not so, Eth?"

Eth stared at her then. Her eyes were vermilion in the firelight, deep, shining, drawing her in. The room seemed to spin round her, Nemony and Vashlian dissolving into shadows, and Eth becoming a watcher inside the old woman's head. Images entered, silent and unbidden. She saw herself grown almost to womanhood, a Guild Mistress wearing a new black gown. She stood beside Nemony in the Council Hall where everyone had gathered to hear her make her vows. All the powers she had she would use to serve them, and the life she lived would be lived for their good and the good of her world. Arlynn smiled and her mother's eyes glowed with pride. And one by one the young men came, Liadd among them, his wild rebellious nature tamed by her own skills, kneeling at her feet and swearing allegiance. And never again would he rage at her and Arlynn, curse and threaten them, or cause her mother pain.

"Yes," murmured Eth. "I would like to be a dreamweaver."

The eyes released her, and the old woman smiled. "Say that again for Nemony, child."

Eth turned towards the woman who would teach her. "I would like to be a dreamweaver, Nemony, truly I would."

Nemony sighed. Her voice sounded sad. "You're

so young, Eth, to accept such discipline and such responsibility. How can you give up your life and your childhood for something you do not understand? And how can I let you? Had you fourteen summers behind you I would not hesitate, but you have only ten. You cannot know what you do. You cannot know!"

"But I still want to," said Eth.

The old woman chuckled. "You see, Nemony? The child is gripped by her own destiny and you cannot dissuade or deny her."

"And who placed it upon her?" Nemony asked curtly.

"Not I," said Mistress Agla. "The child herself and her own dreaming." She heaved to her feet in a rustle of black robes. "And as you are my acolyte on this occasion, Vashlian, fetch me a quill pen and parchment, then saddle my riding jendo. Take this child home with a note for her mother. The Dreamweavers' Guild has found another recruit."

Darkness was falling with sodden leaves and rain, Malroth and the mountains hidden by cloud, when Eth left the cottage. The years of her childhood and conventional schooling were over. She would be given to Nemony as an apprentice as soon as her mother signed the papers. Riding high on the jendo's back and clutching its mane, she could not share Nemony's sadness. She wanted to laugh in triumph, sing with excitement, and the forest was full of scents that thrilled her senses. Rain-beads that spangled the braids of her hair and soaked through her kirtle did nothing to dampen her spirits, and Vashlian, leading her homewards, spoke no word to break the spell.

His soft steps mingled with the woodland sounds – leaf-fall and rain-fall and the wings of owlins, the distant howling of vinx. He would guard her with his life if the need arose. And one day, mused Eth, she would have an acolyte of her own, someone to protect her and care for her, as Brenner did for Nemony, her continued wellbeing his only purpose. Briefly she wondered who he might be and if she would like him – but then the jendo pranced and tossed its head, spooked by the crack of a twig nearby, and Eth would have slipped from the saddle had Vashlian not caught her.

"Pay attention to what you do!" he said crossly. "Arbroth has need of you, girl. Break your neck later, by all means, but don't do it now!"

Obediently, Eth tightened her knees around the jendo's girth and, shortly after, the journey ended at her mother's house. Rain dripped from the eaves as Vashlian hitched the reins onto the front-porch railing, swung her from the saddle and accompanied her into the house. Eyes turned towards her, orange in the lamplight, and she guessed by the expressions on their faces there had been some kind of quarrel. Kanderin looked troubled, Arlynn wild and despairing, and Liadd hostile as usual. Eth was late for the meal. Stew steamed in their dishes as Kanderin left her seat to greet the stranger.

"Is something amiss?"

Heedless of Vashlian, Eth flung off her kirtle. "I'm to become a dreamweaver!" she announced.

Their expressions changed.

"You?" said Arlynn in surprise.

"You're too young," said Kanderin.

"Mistress Agla thinks not," said Eth. "And Nemony's agreed to teach me."

Liadd slammed down his spoon. "That's all we need! A damned interfering dreamweaver in the family! I warn you, Eth. Try anything on me and I'll kill you!"

Lean and sinewy and quick as a mountain catto, Vashlian moved. His hood was thrown back and the light touched his face, scarred from his brow to his jaw and many years older than Liadd. Nor did he wear his head shaven as most acolytes did. His long dark hair was bound with beads and leather thongs. His thin lips twisted and his orange eyes blazed. Kanderin gasped aloud and Arlynn leapt from her seat as Vashlian drew a dagger from his belt and held it at Liadd's throat. His voice was low and menacing.

"Don't even think of it, boy!"

A pallor became visible beneath Liadd's dusky skin.

"My son doesn't mean it," Kanderin said hurriedly.

"Let us hope not," rasped Vashlian. "The punishment for murder in our society is exile to Malroth!"

For once Liadd was intimidated. "I'm not looking to be exiled," he said shakily.

Vashlian nodded and sheathed the knife.

"And Eth won't be living with us anyway," said Arlynn. "She'll be living with Nemony." Her eyes glowed as she went on speaking. "I'll have the bedroom to myself, which means I can choose a husband at next year's marrying fair. Isn't that wonderful!" She came and kissed Eth's cheek. "I'm so pleased for you, Eth."

"And even more pleased for yourself!" muttered Liadd.

Arlynn turned to him. "Why shouldn't I be?" she demanded.

"I pity the poor milksop who marries you!" said Liadd.

"Mayhap he won't be a milksop!" said Arlynn.

"Mayhap he will be stronger than you are and teach you some respect!"

"Better if he teaches you some!" snarled Liadd.

"Stop it! Both of you!" Kanderin said sharply.

With narrowed eyes Vashlian had watched Liadd and listened. Then he shrugged and took the parchment from the inner pocket of his cloak, placed it on the table and turned his attention to Kanderin.

"Mistress Agla requests that you read this document, lady. It is a deed of apprenticeship that needs to be signed in the presence of others. You are advised to consult with your daughter as to her desires and attend with her tomorrow in the Council Hall where the necessary witnesses will be gathered."

"It is true then?" said Kanderin.

"True enough," Vashlian replied.

"I told you it was!" Eth said gleefully.

Vashlian pulled up his hood. His eyes on her face were cruel and loveless. "Remember what I told you," he said.

"I will," Eth promised.

He bowed his acknowledgement. "Then we shall meet again," he told her.

So saying, he turned on his heel and left, closing the door behind him. But his words remained in Eth's mind and her excitement dimmed in an upsurge of fear. For a boy with blue eyes who had died in her dreams she would leave the home she had been born in, leave Nemony and the village, too, one day. Such a small community could not support two dreamweavers. And what had Vashlian meant when he said they would meet again? What did he know of Eth's future?

"Who was he?" Liadd asked angrily. "Who was he to hold a knife to my throat?"

"I presume he was Mistress Agla's acolyte," said Kanderin.

"Really?" said Liadd. "And do the dreamweavers now employ armed henchmen whilst denouncing so loudly all manifestations of violence? What hypocrisy! The whole damned set-up reeks of it! And not a man left in this village, after my father, who dares to defy them! You wait until I'm grown! I'm going to change things round here, and neither Eth nor that witch-woman, Nemony, will stop me!"

CHAPTER FIVE

When the first snow of winter whitened the Edderhorn, Eth packed what few possessions she had and moved into Nemony's cottage. The village men had built an extension room. It had a timber floor and whitewashed walls, a fireplace and a rocking chair and, from the window, a view of the open meadows and the mountains. It was full of new smells: sawn wood and resin, fresh straw in the mattress and sweet dried herbs in a dish on the table. Candles in holders stood on the mantle shelf, tinderbox and tapers in the hearth and a basket of logs beside it, and, on the wall above, a framed embroidered adage that was Nemony's gift. *By their dreams shall ye know them*, Eth read. Tapestry

53

curtains, two woven mats, and the counterpane she and Arlynn and her mother had sewn, added bright splashes of colour.

It was lovely, thought Eth, a whole room to herself after ten years of sharing. Nemony said it was important that she had her own private space and important, also, that she had her own acolyte. An adjoining door opened directly into the small cubby-hole room where he would sleep and, on behalf of the Dreamweavers' Guild, Mistress Agla had promised to send the first one available. Eth hung her spare clothes in the curtained alcove and stowed away her bag.

"Why do I need one?" she asked.

"There are many reasons," Nemony said. "Much of a dreamweaver's work is done in the small hours of morning and during the day you need someone to guard your sleeping. And, if you dream-walk, a sudden awakening can be dangerous, so again you need someone to guard you. And if you are away too long you need someone to call you back and arouse you. Someone to feed you, Eth, when you forget to feed yourself, to keep you from freezing on winter nights and tend your fire, to be there when you awake in the dark loneliness of night where no one else is."

In the clean new room Eth shivered.

"Won't we be here for each other?" she asked.

"Of course," said Nemony. "We can share each other's dreams as I teach you to weave and we can dream-walk together, but that takes practice. Meanwhile, the village keeps me and I have work to do. Where my dream-body goes yours, as yet, will not be able to follow. It will wander where it will until you have learned to control it. And if you, in my absence should…" Nemony paused and shook her head. "Brenner has not the wit to cope with two of us," she said.

Outside in the back yard Eth heard the crank of the windlass as Brenner hauled water from the well. She knew what Nemony meant. Brenner was strong as the yark-bulls used by lowland farmers to pull their ploughs, but he was still a simpleton, not just physically deformed but mentally impaired as well. Sometimes the village children mimicked and taunted him and Eth, as a small girl, had regarded him with a mixture of pity and fear. After years of visiting Nemony's cottage, she simply accepted him now, and life-lessons at school had taught her that people such as Brenner had as much right to a place in the community as anyone else. Yet, knowing the acolyte sent to serve her would likely be handicapped also, she could not help but question.

"Why is it always the Dreamweavers' Guild who

gives homes and employment to people like Brenner?"

"We don't always," said Nemony.

"Usually," said Eth.

"Who else would give Brenner houseroom?" asked Nemony.

"At school we were taught..."

Nemony sighed.

"What is taught to you, Eth, can often be very different from what people in general are prepared to accept, especially in their own homes. Unfortunately, we do not always practise what we preach, and you should know that from your own experience. In general, we believe in non-aggression, do we not? The renunciation of violence is an essential part of our culture. Yet where your brother is concerned, you and your mother and Arlynn accept and say nothing of his behaviour."

Eth chewed her lip.

"Who told you about Liadd?" she asked.

"Vashlian," said Nemony.

"He was even more aggressive," Eth complained. "He threatened Liadd with a knife! A knife held at his throat, Nemony!"

"What Vashlian does is Mistress Agla's concern," Nemony replied. "He is her acolyte, or so she would have us believe, and it is not my place to question him. But Liadd is a member of our community who will one day take his place amongst the menfolk, and that is my concern. So why haven't I been told, Eth? And how long has it been going on?"

Eth sat on the bed edge and hung her head.

Liadd had warned her clearly enough, but already she was about to betray him. "He always had a temper," she said defensively.

"But this is different?" Nemony prompted.

"It's puberty, Kanderin says."

"Ah," said Nemony.

"She says it will pass," said Eth.

"And what do you think?" Nemony inquired.

"I don't know," said Eth. "I don't really know what puberty is, Nemony. I was going to ask you."

Nemony walked to the window.

"As yet you shouldn't need to know," she murmured. "From the details of birth, and death, and sexuality, we prefer to shelter our children. Yet, as a dreamweaver, you will be confronted with the consequences of all three and the need to deal with them... so I suppose I must tell you."

She turned from the window, added logs to the fire and seated herself in the rocking chair. Then, taking the distaff from her belt, she worked on a small wad of shote fleece, spinning the wool through her fingers and her words through Eth's mind.

"It's like this…" Nemony began.

That night Eth lay awake. The wind was wild in the outside darkness – blowing for a blizzard, Brenner had said at supper – and the spent fire flickered with sudden life, setting the shadows dancing on the whitened walls. Doors and rafters creaked and the cottage was full of unfamiliar sounds, but more disturbing still were the things Nemony had told her. Envisioned in her head was all the blood and mess of human bodies, the instincts involved in their pairing, and mating, and breeding, and the attendant tumult of emotions.

Now Eth knew what Arlynn wanted from the marrying fair and what male hormones drove Liadd to rebel. She understood the long ago look between Kanderin and her father… what Zella and Yordan had been doing in hayloft two summers ago… and why the village youths called Yarbeth a strumpet. And the blood would flow from Eth, too, in a few years' time and the urge to mate would drive her. And maybe she would love the one she coupled with and maybe not. Love was a very different subject, Nemony had said, and she had talked long enough for one afternoon.

Eth pulled the counterpane closer round her face. It smelled of home, of Arlynn's skirts dampened with rillrose water before being pressed and the scented ointment Kanderin used to soothe the chaps on her hands. It made Eth long to be there, set a sick need in her stomach and a lump in her throat. And she was unused to sleeping in a room on her own without Arlynn. The surrounding spaces seemed huge and dark and lonely, and Eth did not want to grow and bleed and know some man's body, rut like a shote and suffer the agonies of giving birth. She did not even want to think of it.

At last she rose from her bed and draped a shawl round her shoulders. Snow lay thick over the garden, whirling with the wind against the window pane as she peered through the curtains. There would be no going home tonight, however much she wanted to. But if she went to Nemony's bedroom at least she would not be alone. To guide her way she lit a candle, its small flame bending in the draught as she opened the door. Beyond was a flagstoned hallway, icy beneath her feet, and a lighted oil lamp in the front porch beckoning to anyone who needed shelter.

The sound of the night wind whining outside made Eth shiver, but the kitchen was warmer, the fire in the inglenook still burning brightly. It must have been almost midnight, yet the bench was empty where Brenner usually slept, and she found him in the sitting room, slumped on a floor cushion against the closed door of Nemony's chamber, his twisted bulk preventing her from entering. Staring at him in the candlelight, Eth felt again what she had felt as a child, a mixture of pity and fear. His misshapen head, bald as a baby's, lolled on one hunched shoulder and his cavernous mouth was open in sleep. Drool trickled from his tongue. His ugliness repelled her, but she summoned her courage and tapped him on the shoulder, watched his eyes open, red-rimmed and bleary, and gaze uncomprehendingly up at her.

"Can I come by?" she asked.

His twisted body stirred and he shook his head.

"N-Not...yet," said Brenner.

"I need to see Nemony," Eth insisted.

"M-M...Mistress...N-Nemony...gone."

"Gone?" said Eth. "Gone where?"

"G...gone...see...Z-Zella," stammered Brenner. "G-grieve lost b-baby. D-dream...n-nightmares. M-Mistress...N-Nemony...visiting."

"She can't be," said Eth. "Not in this weather."

"D...dream-walk," said Brenner. "Not...w-wake...yet."

"Oh," said Eth.

"I... h-help...l-little...mistress?"

"No," said Eth. "It's not important."

She returned to her room but she did not try to

60

sleep. Instead she raked the ashes from the fire, added logs and kindling, sat in the rocking chair and stared at the flames. People were not just physical, Nemony had said, not just bones and flesh and blood. They had another body, a dream-body existing inside them that was equally real, although few were actively aware of it. But Nemony slipped from her flesh as a hand from a glove, and her dream-body went travelling. She could go where she willed, regardless of time or distance, the lie of the land or the adverse weather. And so would Eth one day – or maybe now, if she tried. Maybe, if she tried, she could even go home.

She had no idea how to set about it. She simply stared at a flickering point within the fire and wished... stared and wished, without moving or thinking, her lips repeating the same words over and over in a soundless chant. "I want to go home... I want to go home... I want to go home..." The warmth made her drowsy. Her eyelids grew heavy. Far away the wind sang softly and snow brushed soft as sand against the window pane... and the room in the firelight faded with all awareness of her body.

For a moment, there was nothing... only the moan of the wind and a dull red light all around her... a dream drawing her into it, but not the one

61

she wanted. It was not her home she wakened to but another world where the wind tore at her night-shift, tangled her hair and stoppered her mouth with sand. And sand she walked upon, beating her way through stinging ochre mists towards a looming wall that would give her shelter, then groped her way along its crumbling stones to enter the arched gateway of a town.

The wind eased somewhat, yet the sound of it was all she heard, eerily whining through broken doors and windows. The town was in ruins, all that remained of it being slowly buried by sand. She walked through dunes along empty streets and saw nothing alive besides herself. Then, as she crossed a paved square towards the only building that remained intact, she heard the shrill whinnying of jendoes, and the shout of a human voice.

The building, more huge than any Council Hall that Eth had ever seen, was fashioned in white marble with wide flighted steps leading up to a pillared portico. Eroded statues gazed at her blindly from niches in its walls, bestial creations that parodied the human form. And the great door had fallen away, rotted to splinters.

Eddies of sand whispered with the wind up a columned aisle and a group of men, along with their jendoes, were encamped at the far end away from the reach of the storm. Eth could smell the reek of sweat and dung as she approached, although she paid them little heed. Her gaze was fixed on the statue that towered above them – its shote-like thighs, its swollen genitals, its horned head and man-like face. She knew nothing of evil – it was just a word in the Arbrothan language – yet she saw it in the cruel carved eyes that stared into hers.

The men turned towards her. They were robed and hooded, their faces bound for protection so that only their eyes showed – hard eyes, ruthless eyes, bitter and angry in various shades of orange. And Liadd was among them, or maybe it was not Liadd but someone just like him, older and more brutal. Terrified, Eth recognised her father. She had come home after all to the man who had begat her! He moved towards her, a dagger clutched in his hand, and her cry echoed through the vast empty spaces of the building. He was going to kill her, she thought. But there was another man, lither and quicker than he, who stayed his arm.

"She's a dream-image, Aldo! Nothing more!"

"I know what she is!" snarled Eth's father. "But who has sent her, Vashlian? And for what reason?"

Vashlian, Mistress Agla's acolyte! Eth's heart leapt with sudden hope as he pulled back his hood and unwound the drapes from his face. There was the scar she remembered, his loveless eyes fixed on her face in surprised recognition. But his voice grated as the sand on the stones, denying he knew her.

"What brings you to Malroth, girl? And who are you?"

Eth opened her mouth to reply but gently, urgently, someone called her name. She felt it as a tug at her very being, hauling her away through the wind and sand, across the space between worlds into a moment of darkness where she ceased to exist at all. Then there was a jolt of arrival, the heavy tightness of a body closing around her and trapping her inside. When she opened her eyes she was back in the rocking chair beside the fire. Nemony, in her night-shift, was kneeling before her, gripping her hands, and Brenner hovered, agitatedly, in the shadows beyond.

"Don't ever do that again," said Nemony. "Not without telling me, Eth. If Brenner had not heard you cry you could have been lost to this world for ever!"

Eth stared at her, rigid with shock.

Her lips moved but her voice failed to form the questions.

And someone knocked at the outside door.

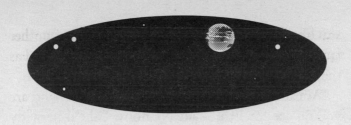

CHAPTER SIX

It was half past midnight when Nemony opened the door and she had no need to ask who stood there. It was obvious, from the grey robes he wore, who he was and why he had come. Snow slipped from his shoulders as he stepped inside, dripped from his hood and his travel bag, melted in pools around his feet. Watching from her room Eth saw the built-up boot and metal callipers, and a shrivelled arm extended in greeting. His name was Cable, he said. He had been sent by Mistress Agla to serve the trainee dreamweaver but the weather had delayed his arrival.

"I expected the village to have a public trans-matt terminal," he said. "Instead, I had to tramp all the way from the nearest town, so if I wakened you, I'm sorry."

"You didn't wake us," said Nemony.

"Am I for you, Mistress?"

"You are for Eth," said Nemony. "She'll be with you in a minute. Go with Brenner, take off your wet things and warm yourself by the kitchen fire, and I'll tell her you're here."

"Not if she is occupied," Cable said hastily.

"She isn't," Nemony assured him. "But she returned only moments before your arrival and needs to compose herself."

Cable nodded his understanding. Then, picking up his travel bag, he followed Brenner into the kitchen and was gone from Eth's view. And in a white swirl of night-robes Nemony re-entered her room. Firelight and candlelight shone in the dreamweaver's eyes and suppressed excitement showed in her smile.

"Your acolyte has arrived," she announced.

"I heard," muttered Eth.

"Do you feel up to meeting him?"

"I don't know," Eth said uncertainly.

Again Nemony knelt before her and gripped her hands. Her voice was soft with sympathy. "Was it so bad an experience, Eth?"

Eth began to cry. "It was horrible!" she sobbed.

Nemony fetched Eth's kirtle from the wardrobe

alcove and draped it round her shoulders. "Come," she said. "We'll go to the kitchen. You can tell it and Cable can share it. It's what he is here for and he may as well begin right away."

Eth sniffed away her tears.

"If you were me would you tell Brenner?" she asked.

"Of course," said Nemony. "Who else do I have who will listen? That's why he is with me, Eth. Although how much he understands is another question. But I suspect Cable has no such limitations. Quite the reverse, I would say."

Eth chewed her lip. There had to be trust between a dreamweaver and her acolyte but she was not sure she wanted to tell her latest dream to some strange man she did not know. It was too personal, almost like showing him her naked body. She was ashamed of its images – the hideous horned statue with its marble genitals and the brute who had fathered her. Reluctantly, fastening her kirtle and pulling on her slipper-socks, she accompanied Nemony to the kitchen. She would tell it differently, she decided, or maybe tell just part of it and not all. But Cable, seated in the inglenook and already supplied with a dish of warmed-up stew, was hardly a man.

Eth gazed at him in surprise and, equally surprised, he gazed at her, the spoon poised halfway to his mouth. He was a youth not much older than Liadd. Light glinted on the smooth shaved dome of his skull, on the fine bones of his face and the small gold stud in his right nostril. And his eyes were not orange but tawny, tawny as owlin feathers and flecked with amber, the most beautiful eyes Eth had ever seen. She felt a flush of shyness and hung her head. His callipers had been discarded, and the black ugly boots he wore for travelling had been set to dry beside the fire. One bare shrivelled foot showed beneath his grey acolyte's gown and Nemony propelled her towards him.

"This is Eth," she said.

Cable frowned, accepted the hunk of bread that Brenner offered him, and frowned again. "She's no more than a child!" he objected.

"And you yourself are younger than I expected," Nemony replied.

"I'm fourteen!" Cable said indignantly. "I'm a fully qualified acolyte and I didn't come here to babysit!"

"I'm not a baby!" Eth protested.

Nemony chuckled. "Indeed you're not," Nemony said softly. "Wherever you were just now, you were not on Arbroth." She turned to Cable. "Can you call back a dream-walker from beyond this planet's aura?" she asked.

Cable gaped at Nemony. "You've trained her to dream-walk already? At her age?"

"I've not yet trained her in anything," said Nemony.

"And you really expect me to believe...?"

"Were you not briefed?" asked Nemony.

The wind whined down the chimney.

Brenner filled the kettle and set it to boil.

And Cable dunked bread in his stew.

"I was told she was a natural," he admitted. "I was told I had to listen to her well and report to the Guild on anything unusual. But I wasn't told why, or how young she was, or what I'm supposed to..." He paused and stared again at Eth. "I was also told... Does she really translate herself back into the physical dimension when she's dream-walking?"

Nemony's hands tightened on Eth's shoulders.

"We don't know what she does," she confessed. "And we don't know how she travels. This is the first experience I've had of Eth's abilities. I only know she was not on Arbroth just now when I and Brenner called her back and wherever she was I was unable to follow. Where did you go, Eth?"

"It was only a dream," said Eth.

"There were no rapid eye movements," said Nemony.

"You mean she can't distinguish?" asked Cable.

"I've told you," said Nemony. "I've not trained her in anything. Whatever Eth experiences at night will seem to her to be a dream."

Eth glanced up at her.

"Are you saying it was real, Nemony? Are you saying I've really been to Malroth? So how did I get there? And how did Vashlian get there? Was he dream-walking, too?"

"Vashlian?" Cable's voice was sharp, and if he was tired from travelling his face showed no trace of it. He set aside his dish and leaned towards her, tawny eyes gazing into hers, intelligent and curious. "What do you know of Vashlian?" he asked.

"He's Mistress Agla's acolyte," said Eth.

"An acolyte?" exclaimed Cable.

"We were led to believe he was," Nemony said stiffly.

Brenner cackled with laughter.

"V-Vashlian...n-no...acolyte," he declared.

"I noticed he was somewhat lacking in deference," murmured Nemony. "Yet it was under that guise he came here and Mistress Agla offered no alternative explanation. Are we allowed to know the reason for such a masquerade?"

Cable frowned.

"I doubt if Mistress Agla even knows," he said. "Vashlian is a law unto himself. It is rumoured that

70

the Guild does not employ him but that he employs the Guild. We think he is a spy from the Institute of Sciences, I and my fellow students at the Academy. But if Vashlian came here in person it must have been important..."

"He questioned me about my dreams," said Eth.

"What dreams?" asked Cable.

And Eth found herself telling him... everything.

After a while Nemony returned to her room to continue her work and Brenner guarded her, but through the small hours of morning Eth and Cable talked. He was older than she, able to explain the difference between dreaming and dream-walking and the underlying significance of her experience. Things connected up in her mind. What she had always known she now understood and her understanding was not that of a child.

She had been taught history at school, the history of Malroth destroyed by atomic war many centuries ago, its cities reduced to rubble, its rich farmlands to desert. She had been taught that many of Malroth's people had escaped to Arbroth through the trans-matt system and begun again – a new world, a new civilisation, fairer, simpler – where none were rich and none were poor, and violence was outlawed, and scientific invention strictly vetted and seldom applied. It was how Eth lived, many generations later, in a small unchanging community ruled by the land and the seasons, where people survived by their own labour, helped each other and shared what they had. But life had not been like that on Malroth, Cable informed her.

"And do you know why?"

"No," said Eth.

"Because it was ruled entirely by men," said Cable. "That statue you saw, a symbol of their power, was El-Tesh, the horned god. He was worshipped there for centuries, an unbalanced religion in which women had no place."

"What's a religion?" asked Eth. "What's worship? What's god? I don't understand the words, Cable."

Cable tried to explain the sense of the numinous and the almighty power of creation. On Arbroth it was acknowledged in the universe itself, in the natural landscapes and the four essential elements, in the wind and the weather and the light of the Roth Star, in plants and animals and people. But on Malroth, people believed that all things came from El-Tesh. His words and wishes, interpreted by priests, became laws that no one could question, and rituals were devised to praise and placate him. This was called worship, said Cable, and anyone who questioned the dictates of the priests, who worshipped in a different way or refused to believe El-Tesh existed either as a god or an entity apart from his image, were persecuted, imprisoned, sacrificed or slaughtered.

On Malroth, in the name of El-Tesh, the priests had assumed power over everyone else. They extracted payment from people for their prayers of intercession, anointed kings who had ruled the population on their behalf, gathered armies to quell rebellions and employed scholars to study science and invent new weapons for killing. And women were considered inferior to men because they lacked male genitalia and were not created in the image of El-Tesh. Women on Malroth had no power, no voice, no human rights, no social status. Unopposed and with the blessings of El-Tesh, the men who ruled were free to commit all manner of atrocities. They built machines to harness and subjugate the forces of nature, and finally they destroyed themselves and the planet.

"Which is why we have no orthodox religion on Arbroth," said Cable. "Why we have no temples, or images, or ritual worship, and recognise no goddess or god. Just lakes and forests and mountains – the sacred landscape and the sacred seasons. It's why we accept women and men to be of equal importance, and why even a child may have a voice. Our only problem is in keeping it that way."

"Why is it a problem?" asked Eth. "Surely it's how things are on Arbroth and how they've always been. We can't live in any other way. So why is it a problem?"

Cable stared at her.

"Don't you know anything about a dreamweaver's work?"

"Nemony hasn't begun to teach me yet," Eth reminded him.

"I'm not talking about techniques," said Cable. "I'm talking about the issues involved, the underlying purpose."

Eth shook her head.

"I don't know," she said.

"You don't know? Even though you're going to be one?" Cable frowned, raked out the fire and added more logs. "That doesn't make sense, Eth! How can Nemony teach you if you don't why you are being taught? And how can you utilise your skills if you don't know what they are for?"

"They're to help people," said Eth.

"But in what way?" asked Cable.

"I don't know," Eth repeated.

Cable watched the new flames leap into life.

"Then I had better tell you," he said.

The storm had lessened, the wind no more than a

whisper beyond the walls, irrelevant and undistracting. All Eth's attention was fixed on the acolyte, his quiet eyes, the inflexions of his voice, his words, his meaning.

The work of a dreamweaver, said Cable, although she dealt with individuals, was to maintain a harmony within the community that employed her, a harmony between women and men. Twenty centuries of tradition had set the pattern for people's lives but problems arose, nonetheless. Social injustices or petty quarrels between neighbours, if left unresolved, could become family vendettas and split the community. Personal jealousies, if they were allowed to flourish, could grow out of all proportion and small confrontations could stir up enough resentment to cause a local war.

And there was always the odd one or two who rebelled against the way things were and determined to live differently. A few who remained driven by their baser instincts, who grew to be corrupt or violent and out of control, a bane to their families and the community in which they lived.

"But who controls the dream, controls the man," said Cable. "And that's what your work consists of. A dreamweaver unravels people's problems, roots out resentment or aggression or whatever other negative drive is apparently operating in a particular man or woman, and restores the balance of their relationships. You dreamweave for the peace of this planet, Eth, that each individual person may learn and understand, grow and forgive. And sometimes you fail. And the failures are the ones who are exiled, sent to Malroth through the trans-matt system – men like your father who allow themselves to be ruled by the violence of their own natures, whose behaviour in one way or another is generally unacceptable. And women, too, who are foolish enough to behave in a similar way, who condone their ways or are willing follow them. The stability of Arbroth rests with its dreamweavers. Now do you understand?"

Appalled, Eth stared at him. She understood, all right. She understood what would happen to Liadd if he put his threat into practice. Things were going to change, he had said. But if Kanderin refused to shield him, if the dreams Eth or Nemony were one day called upon to weave for him failed to temper his ambitions, then he, too, would be exiled to Malroth along with his father. For Liadd's future Eth would become responsible.

It was a huge undertaking for a ten-year-old girl and an equally huge determination gripped her. She could not let anything happen to Liadd, she decided. He was her brother, the one she had tagged behind as a small child, who had taught her to fish and swim and climb trees. He had wiped away her tears when she slipped on the ice-slide, hauled her from a bog on the mountain and carried her home on his back. It was Liadd who had taken her nutting in the woods, defended her from vinxes and owlins and older children, sided with her against Arlynn and her mother over torn clothes, smashed crocks and bad behaviour. He had gone wrong lately, but it was not too late to save him from himself.

"How long will it take?" Eth asked Cable.

"How long will what take?" he inquired.

"For me to become an accomplished dream-weaver?"

Cable regarded her.

Then, wearily, he closed his eyes.

"The rest of your life?" he replied.

CHAPTER SEVEN

They were strange years, the years of Eth's growing.
One day a week she took lessons at the village school,
improving her literacy and numeracy, but she ceased
to have friends there. And once a month she visited
Arlynn and her mother – Liadd, too, if he happened
to be there – but she was no longer a part of the
family. Her home was with Nemony and Brenner
and her only friend was Cable – Cable, with his sharp
acolyte's mind bound to her service, his arm and leg
crippled by some childhood wasting disease. He
became as dear to her as Liadd had once been, but
from everyone else she grew apart. It had to be so,
Nemony said. A dreamweaver must never be
motivated by self-interest or personal involvement.

On summer evenings, girls and boys of Eth's own age romped in the meadows and over the lower slopes of the mountains, roamed through the woods and swam in the lake, but she was never one of them. Her life was taken up with learning the dreamweaver's craft. Nor was she there at the marrying fair when Arlynn chose Hurli to share her bed, although she did attend the wedding feast that autumn as any village dreamweaver would have done. Respect she was shown a-plenty, even from her own peer group, yet because of her age she played no part in the life of the community.

Births, deaths and marryings, and all other affairs of the village, invariably involved the local dreamweaver, too. But the dreamweaver was Nemony. It was she who was called upon to deal with family problems, to confront or allay all the griefs and fears, jealousies and uncertainties that occasionally arose within various close relationships. It was she everyone turned to for healing and counselling and no one was willing to consult with Eth or employ a child to act on their behalf.

Eth was considered too young to be of use, however adept she was. And barred from direct participation, she had no opportunity to practise what she learned, no chance to weave dreams on anyone but Cable and Nemony, and nowhere to dream-walk to. She could only accompany Nemony through the etheric landscape towards a destination she had no permission to enter and a weaving session she was not allowed to share, then wander aimlessly home again.

During the early years of her training Eth did not mind too much. Escaping from her body was enough in itself, a strange and beautiful experience. The first time had made an unforgettable impact on her and changed her whole perception of human existence. She did as she had done on previous occasions when nothing had happened – stared at the flame of a candle, as Nemony had instructed, emptied her mind of thoughts and ceased to be aware of herself. Before, she had never got beyond emptying her mind, for the moment she did so the thoughts returned to plague her, but that night she was tired. A sleepy drifting feeling seemed to wash through her head and she simply went with it, floating effortlessly towards the ceiling, then turned to see her physical self seated in the chair beneath her, a thin silver cord joining her to it. The shock of realisation returned her instantly to a state of wakefulness within her skin, yet now she knew she was not just a body. She was something else, too, immortal and undying, and so were all people, whether or not they owned it.

As she grew more and more accomplished at

dream-walking, able to travel beyond the walls of her room and pass through the various etheric planes that were haunted by ancestral spirits, Eth understood death as part of life. It was a rite of passage – the dream-body finally abandoning its physical shell to live elsewhere – another kind of birth, in a way. She lost her fear of it and never again had nightmares of dying in the trans-matt system, or grieved for the deaths of those who had grown old: Yordan's grandsire drowned in the shote-wash pool and Zuke's mother taken by the winter's cold. Their bodies were burned in Arbroth's fires but somewhere, in the etheric realms, Eth knew they lived on.

In all there were seven etheric planes, Nemony taught her. The physical plane was the lowest and dream-walking was done through the second plane, the auric plane, between the dimension of the so-called living and the so-called dead. Eth could visit the higher planes but she could not stay there and waking usually erased the memory. She was not a medium, as many dreamweavers were. No higher being guided her or chose her as an oracle, took over her body whenever she vacated it and used her vocal cords to speak. Once trained, she would be as Nemony, an ordinary dreamweaver with no special skills.

But to Eth the auric plane was magnificent in itself. Drifting with Nemony towards the village, the familiar landscape changed. Strange bright edges of luminescence surrounded all things. Each leaf and grass blade shone lemony-green with life. Stones glowed russet-red. The sky turned violet. The Roth Star burned white, flamed and flared with gouts of sheer colour, and Malroth smouldered, red as a dying ember. At night the summer woods glowed greeny-golden. Owlins, and minces, and vinxes, became streaks of scarlet moving through indigo shadows beneath the trees. And people were changed too, their physical bodies grey and featureless and indistinct, recognisable only by the auras of light that surrounded them. Cable's was clear pale blue, Nemony's pink, Brenner's orange as his eyes, Arlynn's yellow, Kanderin's green and Liadd's red and fiery, uncertain as his temper.

Eth could never tire of that kind of seeing, never lose her sense of awe and wonder, yet it had little to do with being a dreamweaver. And although she learned to read human auras, could diagnose mood and disease in the variances of colour, she made no attempt to treat it or ease it. She could weave dreams and brew herbal concoctions as competently as Nemony, but she could not practise. Her age, and a general mistrust of her youthfulness, continued to thwart her.

Seasons passed and Eth's frustration increased with her awareness. She grew tetchy and impatient, argued with Nemony and bickered with Cable. She was fourteen years old now, but still the village people saw her as a child and refused to employ her – and each refusal denied her skills and added to her grievances.

Not even Arlynn, visiting the cottage one warm summer evening, was willing to confide in her. Closeted with Nemony in the sitting room, Eth was not privy to what was said, although afterwards, sitting around the supper table, the dreamweaver reported on their conversation. Arlynn was worried about Hurli, Nemony said. Under Liadd's influence he had ceased to show her the respect she considered was due to her, not just as his wife but as a human being. It was how Liadd treated Kanderin, Arlynn had claimed, as if she were some kind of inferior species, although usually Kanderin chose not to see it or else made excuses for him. Out of love for Hurli, Arlynn had tried to do the same. But last night he had struck her and forced himself on her and she could not stay blind any longer. His behaviour was inexcusable and the time had come to do something about it, Arlynn had said.

Listening, Eth felt annoyed and useless. "We

should have done something about Liadd ages ago!" she said crossly.

"We've received no direct complaints about him," said Nemony.

"And why didn't Arlynn consult with me, anyway?"

Nemony looked at her in surprise.

"Did you expect her to?"

"I am her sister!"

"But you are hardly qualified to handle this kind of situation between man and wife, Eth."

"You mean I'm not old enough? So how old must I be then?"

"It has more to do with experience than age," Nemony explained.

"And you don't have the experience," said Cable.

Eth glared at him, and her annoyance turned to anger.

"Well, how am I going to get it?" she demanded. "If I'm not involved in anything and I'm never allowed to practise, how am I going to get it? What's the point in my going on weaving dreams for you and Nemony? You're trained to receive them anyway and they serve no purpose! It's just a waste of time! And a waste of time dream-walking, too! I'd be better off apprenticed to Zella and learning to weave carpets! At least what I did would have a result! As it is I'm no use to anyone and I never will be at this rate!"

Cable leaned towards her. His eyes were gentle in the twilight. "You can't just dive into things, Eth. You have to have the necessary emotional understanding – and that only comes with maturity."

"And how old are you?" Eth asked furiously.

"Old enough to know that you haven't got a clue about what makes a man behave as he does and how a woman feels," Cable replied.

"Yes I have!" Eth argued. "You've been telling me ever since I came here! And so has Nemony!"

"That's not experience," said Cable.

"Maybe next year…?" suggested Nemony.

Eth had heard enough. It was excuses – all of it – Cable and Nemony siding against her, diminishing who she was and everything she had learned. She stormed off into the dusk and slammed the door. Tears of anger shimmered in her eyes and her running footsteps crushed the herbs that overhung the garden path. She barely saw the black-robed figure hobbling up the track. In no mood for ceremonial greetings, she simply ignored Mistress Agla and set out across the freshly mown meadows towards the mountains.

Later, sitting on an outcrop of rock and staring down at the valley, a terrible loneliness oppressed her. She was tired of dreams, tired of wandering alone through the auric plane. Lights from the village shone small as stars in the darkness beneath her – the great black pyramid, the new two-way trans-matt terminal in the square, flooding the cobbles with pale iridescence as its doorway opened. She ached to be down there, to be a part of it all, to dance at the hay-feast tomorrow with others of her age and be accepted again as she had once been accepted as a child. She wanted to be an ordinary girl, weaving dreams for herself of the marrying fair as Arlynn had done, laugh and love, even if it did go sour. But her own unasked-for experiences had trapped her, the unwanted out-of-body trip of four years ago, the meeting with her father on Malroth and the boy who had died in the trans-matt terminal somewhere in the starry sky.

She raised her eyes. Was he still there? she wondered. His last breath frozen to patterns of ice on his glass sarcophagus? She watched, but nothing moved among the dark infinite spaces. The stars stayed twinkling and motionless however long she stared, and her loneliness remained... loneliness and lovelessness and the great red orb of Malroth hanging low in the west, her link with it that she could never undo.

With a sigh, Eth took the peat road back down the mountains. And there, beyond the next bluff on another outcrop of rock, sat Cable. Stones, disturbed by his boots, rattled down the scree slope as he rose to meet her.

"Are you all right, Eth?"

Her voice was sharp. "How long have you been there?"

"Does it matter?" he asked.

"How did you find me?"

"It's part of my job," he replied.

She waited and he limped to join her. They walked down the peat road together.

"I might have gone to the lake," she said.

"Then I would have found you there," said Cable.

"How?" she repeated.

"Telepathy," he said.

"What?" said Eth.

Cable chuckled.

"Didn't you realise? All acolytes are telepaths. We have to be. How else could we keep track our dreamweavers when they dream-walk? You can go where you will, Eth, but I have only to think of you to know where you are."

Eth stared at him. "You mean I'm never alone? Not ever?"

"Only if you want to be," said Cable.

"That's why I came here!" Eth said angrily.

"Don't worry," Cable said soothingly. "The

psychic link between an acolyte and his dreamweaver is for business purposes only and I know when not to intrude. Why else would I have been sitting where I was?"

She slowed her step to match his limp. It was one thing for his mind to track her when she dream-walked, but he had trailed her with his body, climbed miles in the dark with his crippled leg to sit on a stone and wait.

"What made you come after me anyway?" she asked.

"To tell you Mistress Agla has arrived. She says you are to dreamweave at once, regardless of your age and experience. So with Arlynn's permission and under Nemony's supervision, you'll begin your practice on Hurli – the night after tomorrow, I think."

Eth's eyes shone.

She had won her point.

CHAPTER EIGHT

Hurli was a lively, stocky young man, his brown skin darker than most. He had been born in a distant village, the son of a skilled carpenter who had taught him the trade. Along with other eligible young men of a similar age, he had joined the marrying fair and travelled the land – until Arlynn chose him. Eth could understand why. With his black hair cropped at shoulder length, his quiet manners and merry smile, Hurli had the ability to charm most people, and had Eth been older then she might have envied Arlynn.

At first the marriage had been happy. Hurli had been eager to please both his wife and his adopted mother, had helped Arlynn tend the garden, had carted firewood from the forest and had even cooked the occasional meal. He found a place in the community, too, assisting Zuke in his workshop and doing odd jobs around the village in his spare time. He fixed widow Olna's broken shutter, repaired garden gates, replaced rotting doors and window frames and woodwormed floorboards, and the whole of Kanderin's front porch. He was eager to please everyone, in fact, and Liadd was no exception.

Approaching the age of majority, Liadd was a great strapping youth, half a head taller than Hurli. Unattached to any woman and free to do as he would once the gates to the stone-mason's yard closed at the end of each afternoon, Liadd had scoffed at Hurli's entrapment and scorned his devotion to Arlynn. In Liadd's eyes, Hurli had been little more than a slave, and no self-respecting man played skivvy to a woman, he had said. It was time Hurli became master in his own home and put Arlynn in her place. Women preferred *strong* men, Liadd claimed, men who knew their own minds and knew what they wanted, made decisions and refused to be swayed, not weak-willed wimps such as Hurli.

"And Hurli believed him!" Arlynn said bitterly.

"In a way it's true," said Nemony. "No woman wants a man who is weak-willed. But maybe you, Arlynn, have a different concept of male strength?

Maybe you have been yearning ever since childhood for a man such as your father and you chose Hurli for that very potential?"

Arlynn shook her head.

"I know the difference between strength and brutality!" she claimed. "I don't want a man like my father, Nemony. I don't want to be dominated and beaten into submission. It may be my mother's wish, but it's not mine!"

"Have you talked with Hurli?" Nemony asked.

"I tried," said Arlynn. "But he refused to acknowledge there is anything wrong between us or that he is in any way at fault. He accused me of nagging and provoking him, of denying him sexual favours and not being a proper wife."

"Is he right?" questioned Nemony.

Arlynn glanced at Eth, as if she were not quite comfortable in her presence. Then, regardlessly, she shrugged her shoulders.

"I have begun to nag," she admitted. "Because Kanderin and I do everything and he does nothing. And yes, I do deny him, when he demands and I have no desire. What else should I do? Accept what is unacceptable, as my mother once did, and pretend that all is well?"

Nemony shook her head. "I would not advise any woman to do that, Arlynn."

"You'll help me then?"

"Of course she will," Eth said impulsively.

"Not necessarily," Nemony contradicted.

Eth stared at her in disbelief. "But I thought you said—"

"It takes two to create a problematical relationship," Nemony reminded her. "We have to be satisfied Arlynn does not accuse unjustly. It's all too easy to point the finger and blame another for our own unhappiness, and what she has told us cannot be corroborated. Kanderin will confirm nothing. What takes place between a man and his wife is none of her business, she informed me. And Arlynn's bruises could have been come by in some other way. Can we really impose treatment on Hurli without his knowledge, permission or co-operation, on her say-so alone? And what has Arlynn herself to learn from the situation?"

Bright tears shone in Arlynn's eyes. "Are you saying you don't believe me?" she asked.

"Not necessarily," Nemony repeated.

"Then why are you casting doubt?" Eth asked angrily. "Arlynn's my sister! I've known her all my life…"

"Quite," said Nemony. "And that makes you prejudiced in her favour, does it not? Predisposed to believe whatever trumped-up tale she may tell you?"

Eth's anger blazed into fury. "I don't understand you, Nemony! Arlynn's no liar! She wouldn't make up something like this! I know she wouldn't! And so do you! And if you won't do anything to help her, then I will!"

Arlynn looked at her hopefully. "Would you really, Eth?"

"I'll come tonight," Eth said firmly.

Nemony rose to her feet.

"You will go tonight under my supervision only," the dreamweaver said curtly. "And that is providing Arlynn agrees." She rested her hands on Arlynn's shoulders. "I have been hard on you, and for that I am sorry. I did so primarily that Eth might learn – and you also, my dear. Life sends to each of us the experiences we need in order to grow and develop. In this Hurli is your teacher and you are his, and who are we to judge him? If I am to weave dreams for him, Arlynn, then I must also weave dreams for you, that you may both be strengthened by the situation. Will you comply with this?"

Arlynn stared unseeingly at the stool where Eth was sitting. The bruise on her cheek had already faded and a flush of rose showed beneath her dusky skin. She was angry, thought Eth, at Nemony's cruel interrogation. But the hands of the dreamweaver kneaded her gently, and her lower lip trembled, and suddenly she wept.

"For Hurli's sake I will undergo anything I have to," Arlynn sobbed. "It's him I'm thinking of really, not myself. I love him dearly but I can't bear what he's becoming. Please help him."

"And what of Liadd's part in this?" asked Nemony. "Will you not ask help for your brother, too, Arlynn? Surely if you lodge a complaint against Hurli for allowing himself to be dominated, you must also level an equal complaint against the one who dominates? Mistress Agla will be staying here for another day or so. We could go to her together, ask her advice..."

Arlynn shook her head, raked her long dishevelled hair from her face and dashed a hand across her eyes.

"No," she said fearfully. "Leave Liadd out of it, Nemony."

"Why?" asked the dreamweaver.

Arlynn chewed her lip, and fresh tears shimmered in her eyes.

"I'm afraid of him," she murmured. "I'm afraid of what he might do to me if he ever suspected I had reported him. He could kill me, Nemony, and Kanderin would never forgive—"

"Surely you exaggerate?" said Nemony. "I accept that Liadd has always been quick-tempered and difficult but I cannot imagine him losing his self-control to that extent."

Arlynn's voice broke.

"You don't know what he's like!" she wept. "He's cruel and bullying and he doesn't care how much pain he inflicts or on whom! He screws my wrists, and pulls my hair, and I have seen him beat—"

"Hush," said Nemony. "Hush, Arlynn. He cannot hurt you here."

It was no longer Eth's scene. Arlynn's tears and Nemony's comfort made her redundant. She left the sitting room wondering what exactly she *had* learned from her first interview as a dreamweaver. Arlynn was hurting – Eth could actually feel her torment like a raw wound within herself. Arlynn ought to hate Hurli, not love him. She ought to despise him for the fool he had become. She ought to want to hurt him as he had hurt her – and Liadd, too, regardless of her fear. All the child-love Eth once had for her brother and brother in law evaporated into a feeling of disgust.

Simmering with unexpressed rage on Arlynn's behalf, she picked up the pestle and mortar and crushed the dried heart-shaped leaves of dreamwort to a fine powder. It was a soporific which, added to Hurli's food or drink, would prolong the time spent dreaming and ensure he did not wake. And if Arlynn could not, then Eth would do it – inflict on him an equal torment, a fitting punishment, a just revenge. She would weave a nightmare Hurli would never forget... and afterwards she would begin to practise on Liadd.

Arlynn opened the bedroom window and crept away to spend the night in the kitchen. It was the pre-arranged signal that Hurli slept. Together Eth and Nemony drifted in from the night.

Seen from the auric plane, the room Eth had once shared with Arlynn was no longer familiar. It was an almost lifeless space, a dull grey surround of floors and walls. The timber and stone (of which the room was built) retained but a shadow of the living forests and mountains from where it came, and the fabrics and furniture showed only a faint trace of the hands that had fashioned and tended them, mere shapes against the background, polished patches of ghostly sheen and silken stitchery devoid of colour. Only the flowers glowed, freshly picked and heavy with scent, greeny-gold and iridescent on the bedside-table – and Hurli himself.

His physical body was dim and dimensionless, but his aura was yellow and clear as a sleep crystal, except for some dark feathery strands, cloudy as nimbus, around his skull. Gazing down at the vague impression of his face, Eth's throat suddenly constricted. The fierce hatred of the afternoon and all thoughts of revenge had subsided during the castigation Nemony had given her. To assume someone else's emotions as her own, and be willing to act upon them, was nothing short of foolishness, Nemony had said. Feelings were temporary anyway and not to be trusted. They could become their opposite in the blink of an eyelid and had no place in a dreamweaver's work. Eth should remember, if she accompanied Nemony that night, that she was dealing with a human being as deserving of respect as any other person. And, gazing down at the yellow nimbus of light that flowed from Hurli's true self, Eth experienced a respect bordering on awe.

"He's not evil at all," she exclaimed.

"People seldom are," said Nemony.

"Even though he has behaved as he has done?" asked Eth.

"Wrong action springs from errors of thinking," said Nemony. "Have you never said or done something you regretted, Eth? Never made a mistake? Or acted rashly or foolishly?"

It was a barbed remark intended to put her in her place. She had to remember that she was the trainee and Nemony the dreamweaver, and it was only on Mistress Agla's insistence that she was here at all.

Under Nemony's instruction, Eth began to remove the psychic strands that marred Hurli's aura. Sticky as sugar-fluff sold at the travelling fairs, they stuck to her fingers and invaded the grass-green flares of her own aura. Momentarily she felt their influence, murky and unpleasant, until she shook them away. And as she removed them others arose to take their place, seeping like smoke from the unseen source in Hurli's mind.

It must have taken her an hour or more to clear them. Dark spider-web threads littered the grey auric floor around the bed, were caught by the breeze that blew through the window and carried away. And much of Eth's energy went with them, leaving her tired and depleted, although she had hardly begun the real work of the night.

"You've allowed yourself to become too involved and too intense," Nemony informed her.

"How else should I be?" asked Eth.

"I've told you before: it is necessary for a dreamweaver to remain impersonal. You need to maintain an emotional distance between you and your subject. Also you forgot to erect a protective barrier around yourself, and fatigue is the result. You cannot afford to give of your own energy, Eth. Had you been working within close range of a grossly unhealthy aura and left yourself open, then you would have been really badly affected. And had Hurli happened to be one of those rare malignant souls who actively leech away other people's energy then you would have been risking psychic collapse."

Chastened, Eth rectified the situation. Pale flames burned briefly at her unspoken command, coalesced to a shield of etheric energy that surrounded her. And from within the pink light of her own protected aura, Nemony nodded her approval.

"Are you able to continue?"

"Yes," said Eth.

They took a stance on opposite sides of the bed, watching the shadowy contours of Hurli's physical face, the paler highlights of forehead and cheekbones and the hollows of darkness that contained his eyes. And a length of time passed before the rapid movements of his closed lids indicated he was dreaming.

"Begin when you will," Nemony instructed.

Eth's heart hammered in sudden fear. This was it – the moment she had been waiting for – when she would make connection with another human mind and weave a dream for real. It was a simple enough process. She had merely to supplant Hurli's dream with one of her own making, transmit a pre-arranged sequence of images into his unresisting mind. Yet, as the moments ticked away, the enormity struck her of what she was about to do, and she did nothing. Who controlled the dream controlled the man, Cable had told her. And what right did she have to intrude into someone's head? What right did she have to try and coerce people into changing their behaviour? Could she really do this to Hurli without him even knowing?

"Do you want me to take over?" asked Nemony.

"No," said Eth.

She closed her eyes. If she did not do it, Nemony would. And better a dream that would heal Hurli's heart than have him go ever more wrong. For his sake her dream-mind reached for his, sank deeper and deeper into the dark subconscious depths where all minds were one. And there, indivisible from Hurli, Eth began to weave the dream that she and Nemony had designed in advance.

Arlynn stamped her foot. Her voice was angry and what she said or asked of him was not important. All that mattered was Hurli's own response, the position Arlynn placed him in and what Liadd would think of him if he should give in to her. And his anger was wilder than hers, a man's anger, blazing mad and full of searing resentment – and she the cause of it. With the flat of his hand he struck her hard across the face and her head hit the fender as she fell.

He stared at her then, lying motionless at his feet in a pool of her own blood. A pallor spread beneath her dusky skin and her unseeing eyes gazed up at him. His anger turned to fear. Sick and trembling, Hurli knelt beside her, felt for her pulse and found no trace. Arlynn was dead... and he had killed her... her blood on his hands that he could not wipe away. The tears he would weep, and all the anguish of his remorse, would never absolve him of his crime or alleviate his guilt.

On the bed, Hurli moaned and cried. His breathing was harsh and sweat dewed his physical body with little sparkles of light. The dream should have ended there, the lesson it contained complete in itself. But the images continued to flow, rising unbidden from the vast depths of the communal mind, and Eth failed to quell or control them. The dream went on...

People came from the village and dragged Hurli away, held trial in the Council Hall and condemned him for murder to a life of exile. The great black pyramid of the trans-matt terminal swallowed him up and spat him out in some other place where no one was. Outcast for ever, alone and friendless, he wandered the deserts of Malroth, crying for Arlynn and bitterly repenting of what he had done. But there was laughter in the wind, laughter in the blowing sand: Liadd, who had mocked and scorned him and incited him to kill, stood before him and laughed at his plight.

Hurli clenched his fists. Mad with hatred he knew he would kill Liadd then – but Liadd suddenly changed. His limbs became shote's legs, his flesh became stone, curled horns sprouted from his forehead. Leering and malevolent, the monstrous marble statue gazed down on Hurli. And the eyes and soul of it were Liadd's... and the laughter was Liadd's... and there was nothing Hurli could do.

Far away, on a bed in a room, Hurli's physical body thrashed in the grip of his dream. The vase of flowers on the beside table toppled and fell. Eth heard the crash, saw bright water pooling on a distant floor and somewhere in the grey surrounding mist Nemony spoke. Eth did not hear what she said. The dream was hers, too, its reality whipping her away. She was light as thistledown being hurled through a vortex of wind and sand. Her shriek echoed Hurli's and was lost beyond the boundaries of her world where no one could follow.

CHAPTER NINE

Cable hauled on the thin silver cord that bound Eth to her physical body. Wind and sand fled to memory and she was back in the auric plane, its lights and colours hurtling past her. Then she awoke with a sickening lurch inside the tightness of her skin. Her stomach heaved. Pain pounded in her head. Dawn light beyond the window, and the summer heat, seared her eyes and deprived her of breath. Retching, gasping, pouring with sweat, she toppled from the rocking chair into Cable's arms.

"For crying out loud!" yelled Cable. "That was a dreamweaving session you were at! You weren't supposed to go wandering off across the galaxy, Eth!"

"I feel sick," she moaned.

It was his fault. The sudden return, the sudden awakening, had shocked her whole body–mind system. He fetched a bowl and sponged her face and arms with rillrose water, made a compress for her head, drew the curtains and put her to bed. He asked no questions because she was in no state to answer – and she would never know how much she had scared him. Sitting guard on a stool outside her door, Cable waited until Nemony completed the dreamweaving session and returned to her own body. Distraught and dishevelled, bare-footed and semi-clad, with Brenner behind her, she came running into the hallway.

"Is Eth all right?"

Cable nodded.

And when Nemony checked, she was already asleep.

Raised voices wakened her hours later. Closed curtains made a darkness in the room but the door was ajar to let in the air and the gold light of evening filled the hallway beyond. Remnants of the previous night's pain still throbbed in her head. And it was she they talked of, Nemony, Mistress Agla and Cable.

"How could she do such a thing?" Nemony said angrily.

"It was hardly likely to be deliberate," demurred

Mistress Agla.

"Had it not been for Cable—"

"She took me by surprise," said Cable. "I wasn't expecting it and I wasn't exactly gentle. I just reacted..."

"No one's accusing you," said Nemony.

"It happened so quickly," said Cable. "One moment she was where she should have been and the next moment she was thousands of miles beyond the orbit of Arbroth. And she actually translated out of the auric altogether."

"Faded," said Nemony. "Before my very eyes!"

"Had anyone been there she would have been visible," said Cable.

"And after all the times I've told her!" Nemony said crossly.

"It's for that capacity, among others, that we have need of her," said Mistress Agla.

"That's as maybe," Nemony retorted. "But it is of no use in the work of a village dreamweaver! Quite the reverse! Become visible in some man's bedroom and the whole Guild will be brought into disrepute!"

The old woman chuckled. "I hardly think Eth is representative—"

"She is as far as this locality is concerned!" Nemony said curtly. "And I have my own reputation to think of! Eth could be our ruination around here, Mistress Agla. If treatments go wrong, or turn out badly, then who will come to us? And who will trust us? And what will be the impact on our culture? We could foster a rebellion in this village! And I dread to think what the consequences will be of last night's fiasco!"

"Mayhap no ill will come of it," murmured Mistress Agla.

"It should not have happened!" Nemony went on. "The dream Eth weaved had been pre-arranged, yet she made no attempt to end it or control the continuing upsurge of images. Nor did she attempt to select those that were appropriate to the young man in question. She simply disregarded his needs, allowed herself to be overwhelmed and he along with her!"

"When confronted by an archetype even a practised dreamweaver may experience difficulty," Mistress Agla said soothingly. "They are powerful and dangerous, Nemony, as you well know. And El-Tesh is no exception. He is the bane of our race-memory, the ultimate horror. Can we really blame the child for such an unfortunate encounter?"

Cutlery rattled, and stew smells drifted in from the kitchen.

"She has encountered El-Tesh before," said Cable.

"And she's no longer a child," added Nemony.

"Besides, she has practised on Cable and I often enough to know the blocking techniques. According to your instructions, Mistress Agla, I have taught her all I can of the dreamweaver's craft, and I am not intending to blame her for what has happened, but she is far too immature and far too emotional to be allowed to practise on other people. Against my better judgement I let you persuade me, but I won't do it again. In consideration for my clients and in consideration for Eth as well, I am not prepared to employ her again until she has reached the age of majority."

The old woman sighed. "You will grant her no second chance, Nemony?"

"That was my final word," said Nemony.

There was a moment of silence where Eth waited and listened. Outside, the mountain larks sang in the sky and a breath of wind rustled the leaves of the tartfruit tree. The sound of Brenner's axe chopping kindling came from the yard behind the cottage.

"I could order you," Mistress Agla said softly.

"Then I would resign," Nemony replied.

"So where does that leave us?" asked Cable.

The silence returned, and a feeling close to despair filled the emptiness in Eth's stomach, a great lump of rejection worse than the pain in her head. Tears of mortification slid down her cheeks. She was condemned as a failure and would be cast out of the Dreamweavers' Guild before she had even been accepted. The kitchen door slammed in the breeze and she heard nothing more – but the sunlight darkened and her future, it seemed, was no longer with Cable and Nemony and Mistress Agla.

After a while Eth dressed in her sleeveless blue day-shift, brushed and braided her long dark hair, then, stuffing a pillow under the sheet to represent her sleeping body, she closed the bedroom door quietly behind her and let herself out of the house. She could not face them, she thought, and nor could she face the awfulness of her own disgrace. She needed time to think and recover, and she needed to be alone.

It was late in the evening. Mountain shadows were long and deep, the sky drained and colourless, the land baked dry from the summer's heat. She might have headed for the Edderhorn, but last time she had been there Cable had found her, so she chose the forest instead. The massed trees camouflaged her aura, her life force lost among the myriad life-forces around her. The flickering shade somewhat consoled her and the scent of earth was sweet and strong. She wended her way along the verndeer trails to emerge at nightfall on a wooded promontory that jutted into the lake.

The water shone russet red, reflecting Malroth's light, and the Roth Star had set behind the mountains, tingeing the sky with fiery hues. As the twilight deepened, it was Malroth that held her eyes, its great orange–red orb hanging low above the horizon. Malroth, barren and forsaken, a place of exile – and she was connected to it, connected by her blood and body to a man she hated, the only connection she had left.

Tears prickled her eyes. No one remained for her on Arbroth. The bonds that had bound her as a child to her mother and Arlynn had been broken long ago – and her love for Liadd had been destroyed. And now Cable and Nemony were lost to her. Dismissed from the dreamweaver's service, stripped of her role and robbed of her purpose, she would live out her life alone in the village in accommodation allotted out of kindness – and all she needed and all she possessed would be given in charity to one who had failed to earn a place in the community. They would find her token work to do: household chores, perhaps, for those who were old and infirm – but nothing that meant anything to her. And she would never know why, as a child, she had dream-walked among the unknown stars. She would simply live with the memory of a blue-eyed boy from another world until she, too, died.

Out on the darkening water, marsh fowl cackled and honked, sounds like laughter from the throat of night. And Malroth grew brighter, dimming the surrounding stars. That was where Liadd would end up, Eth thought bitterly, following his father into exile for a crime he had yet to commit, unless someone prevented him. But Kanderin endured, and Arlynn was afraid of him, and Nemony would do nothing without an official complaint. And what was the point of weaving a dream for Hurli while Liadd remained as a source of corruption? On a futile exercise Eth had wrecked her life. Or had she?

Maybe, she thought, it was not too late to put things right. If she could prove herself capable and weave a dream for Liadd that would cause him to change his behaviour, then Nemony might not dismiss her. She clutched at the idea and her heart thumped with sudden nervousness, but it was the only chance she had. She would do it now, she decided, this very night.

She sat in the summer darkness planning the dream and dreaming the plan, occasionally slipping from her body to test the ether for any hint that Cable might be linked to her. But the auric plane stayed empty, except for a distant figure drifting towards the village: Nemony, with the pink nimbus of light shimmering round her, bound for a dreamweaving session. Hastily, Eth returned to the lakeside, moved to sit beneath a clump of willan trees where her own green aura would be less detectable. And all she had to do then was wait, wait until Malroth reached its zenith and Liadd was sure to be asleep. Then, with a final shift from her physical body, Eth departed.

Thinking of Liadd drew her towards him, in through the open window to the grey room that contained him, a shadow shape sprawled on the bed. She had come to save herself, her career and her pride, but the moment she saw him her intention changed. His aura had been scarlet once, clear and shining when she first began to see. Now the red was almost consumed by the black cloudy strands that leaked from his body and his mind. Horrified, Eth stared at him and the sight moved her to pity. Poor Liadd, it was a desperate state he was in – psychically damaged, his dream-body despoiled and even his soul gone dim.

She approached the bed and bent to observe him – the dark wells of his eye sockets, the gash of his mouth. She could smell ale on his breath and feel the influence of his aura. It was seething and hostile, almost malevolent, stirring up a sickness within her and a sense of dread. The black filaments smoked and writhed as if they were alive and she could smell

111

them, too, a putrid nauseating stench. Eth gagged, wanted to withdraw, but she was bound to clear them away before she could begin to dreamweave.

Wrapping herself in a protective shield of light, she gathered up her courage and reached out her hand to touch. And Liadd awoke – not the flesh and blood Liadd she had always known, but the psychic counterpart. His open eyes blazed, no longer orange but red as balefire, gazing at her from the shadows of his face and knowing who she was. He was still trapped within his body, but not for long. Before Eth had time to think or act, his limbs sloughed their skin like snakes and his dream-shape extricated itself, rose from the bed to confront her.

It was the most terrifying experience of Eth's life. Liadd was barely human any more, just a twisted bestial parody of his physical self, snarling and ferocious. Clawed hands grasped the silver cord that bound her to her physical body and hauled her towards him. Spittle flew as he screamed at her.

"What are you doing here, you interfering yark-cow? Thinking to play your tricks on me, were you? Have me wake up different as Hurli did? He was as I wanted him to be! I led and he followed! And now he hates me! He hates me, Eth! And that's your doing! Now you're going pay for it!"

Eth felt the cuff of his hand hard against her mind.

Her defences collapsed and he wound the silver cord round her neck and began to strangle her. His power grew. He seemed to feed from her energy, sapping and depleting her. Darkness boomed in her head. Using the last scrap of strength she had, Eth translated from the auric plane to the physical plane in the hope of escaping him.

It was something Liadd had not learned to do. He had to return to his everyday body and she had time enough to breathe again, time enough to scream before he grabbed the ewer from the wash-stand and hurled it towards her with all his psychic force. It smashed through her, shattered against the opposite wall, and a great bolt of darkness knocked her senseless, blasted her away.

She was not to witness what happened next. She was not even there when Nemony came from Arlynn's room in answer to her cry. Neither did she see when Hurli and Kanderin, awakened by the sound of breaking pottery, came running into Liadd's bedroom, nor the stab of Hurli's knife to Liadd's chest and the bright spurt of Liadd's arterial blood. Deprived of consciousness and lacking the energy to return to her physical body, the darkness took her where it would.

CHAPTER TEN

She survived as a tiny scrap of immaterial existence, a fragile essence of a being who had once been Eth. Formless and shapeless as an embryo, attached to a frail silver umbilicus light-years long, she slept without knowing, blown by the cosmic winds through a darkness without time. And slowly, slowly, she recovered, a battered soul feeding on the universal energy that sustained all life. Slowly, out of unseen light, that soul re-built its aura, spun a cocoon of gold–green luminescence around itself and began to re-create the dream-body that had been destroyed. It budded arms and legs, face and features, reclaimed the memories and experiences that had given it identity. And Eth awoke, drifting across space between the stars.

She thought, at first, she must be dreaming, but then she recalled her brother and the blast of psychic power that had felled her. She could still feel the effects of the damage, the drifting lassitude within her mind that was impossible to fight against. And the silver thread that bound her to her physical body was stretched almost to invisibility, brittle as a human hair that would break at the slightest touch. She was too far away to sense where the rest of her was, and the stars surrounded her, very near and very bright, undimmed by the effects of atmosphere. No familiar constellations. No sign of the Roth Star and the twin worlds spinning around it, nor Cable's telepathic voice calling her home. But something drew her, some unknown influence hauled her across the galaxy towards it.

Such grim events had never before happened in the village at the foot of the mountains. Children squabbled, and could be cruel and unkind before they learned better. And, occasionally, bad feelings developed between friends and neighbours, husbands and wives. And fists flew, now and then, between young men who grew to be rivals, before they left to join the marrying fair. But there had never been a stabbing.

People woke from their sleep as Kanderin ran screaming through the streets to widow Olna's house and begged her aid for Liadd's injury. And a short time later Brenner, the simpleton, roused members of the village Council from their beds. Gathered in the Council Hall, they waited for Nemony and the old Guild Mistress to join them and listened in horror as the dreamweaver made her accusations.

The debate as to what should be done was necessarily brief. Few had much sympathy for Liadd. He was an unpleasant young man and an unsavoury influence, as was his father before him, yet Hurli must be tried for attempted murder. And it was too soon to say what damage Liadd had inflicted on his younger sister, but he would be tried, too, once he recovered. Their first concern was for Eth herself, last seen in Liadd's room.

Apart from Nemony and Mistress Agla, no one on the village Council understood the intricacies of dreamweaving, but the fact that the girl's acolyte was unable to trace her and both women were concerned for her life was motivation enough. At Zuke's request, most able-bodied people – excluding Hurli who had already been apprehended and locked in the wine cellar at the Tavern – gathered in the village square. Search parties left at dawn, combing the forest and the mountain slopes and the margins of the lake as Mistress Agla and Nemony, and Cable, too, in his own different way, continued to search the auric plane for what could only be described as Eth's ghost.

It was several hours later when a group of fishermen found her physical body, a girl in a blue shift lying beneath a clump of willan trees on the promontory. They thought at first that she had drowned, but she lacked the signs. Her limbs were warm and her clothes and hair were dry, her eyes closed as if in sleep. They felt the faint flutter of her pulse and saw the almost imperceptible rise and fall of her chest that proved she breathed. She was alive – just – but they could not rouse her. She remained in a coma from which she would not wake. And although they had been told her brother was responsible for her condition, they could find no injury to account for it, no blow to her head, no wound or abrasion, bruise or blood.

Mindful of the dreamweaver's warning that any sudden movement might reduce Eth's chances of recovery further, they made a stretcher from willan poles and fishing net and carried her to her mother's house. But Kanderin was bitter and refused to receive her, blaming her for all that had happened, and Arlynn was distraught at the arrest of her husband, openly weeping and unable to cope. With the village almost empty of people the fishermen had no other choice. They carried her along the forest track to the dreamweaver's cottage.

Nemony was pale from her nocturnal wanderings and tired from all the exertions of the past few hours. Dark shadows ringed her eyes and worry lines creased her brow and her dusky skin seemed almost translucent in the bright light of day. But her smile was thankful and the fishermen heard the relief in her voice as they followed her into the room some of them had once helped to build.

"They've found her, Cable!" Nemony announced.

Awkwardly the lame acolyte rose from his stool by the bed, and the old woman, seated in the rocking chair beside the empty grate, smiled and nodded. Carefully, without being told, the group of men transferred Eth's body from the stretcher to the bed and shuffled their feet self-consciously before taking their leave.

Cable hardly heard them go – just the scuff of their sandals on the floor. Seated on the stool beside the bed, he was already at work, searching for the thread that bound Eth to her body, the tenuous connection to physical life that would lead to her actual whereabouts. Once he had found her he could haul on the silver cord and bring her back, or else forge the familiar telepathic link to guide her. It would only take a few minutes – or so Cable thought.

Between the stars there was no sensation of speed. The thing seemed to hang there motionless, a shape in the darkness, small at first but growing more and more huge as Eth drifted towards it. It was like a giant beetle, sheened with ice or star-shine, its head a hemisphere of yellow light connected by a slim bridge to a shadowy thorax pitted by rows of blue glass eyes with the black bulk of its abdomen dragging behind. Closer she came, and it grew as she diminished, until she was small as a gnat beside it, a dream-body weightless and substanceless, held there by its gravitational pull. Cold metal walls towered towards the stars above and beneath her, and somewhat below, and to one side, a row of round windows showed a dim blue light from within.

Using her hands as thrusters, Eth propelled herself towards them, breathed away the skin of ice that encrusted the glass and peered inside. And suddenly she understood. The scene was familiar – the blue light, the metal stairs and gantries, the rows and rows of glass sarcophagi. She had returned again to the tomb where her dreams had begun and she recognised it now for what it was – an alien catafalque travelling through space, the turquoise world it came from four years gone. And within it they were not all dead.

Eth watched as a man in a white coat turned the dials and opened the lid of the nearest sarcophagus. Yellow light flowed outwards, and the boy lay within it, perfectly preserved, his face pale as Eth remembered it, his blue eyes closed in death. A long forgotten sorrow touched her heart. She would have liked to know him, she thought. Then, suddenly, his limbs twitched and his dead eyes opened and she saw he was alive. For a moment she did not know what she felt – a little leap of gladness, perhaps, that fled as the meaning struck her. If the boy was alive then so must they all be – hundreds of alien people frozen in sleep and waiting to be revived. And where were they going? she wondered. And what was *she* doing there?

Cable rose from the bed. Light from the sinking Roth Star flooded the room, glinted on the gold stud in his nostril and his smooth, shaved scalp, exposed the tears in his eyes. His lower lip trembled and he had to swallow hard in order to speak.

"She's gone," he said.

"Dead?" Nemony flew to the bedside. "Oh Cable, she can't be!"

Cable swallowed again. "She's way beyond my reach," he said. "So she may as well be dead. I can't bring her back, Nemony."

"But you've got to!" said Nemony. "She will die

for sure if you don't! Flesh needs food and drink to sustain it and we can't keep her body alive indefinitely! You must keep trying, Cable!"

Cable dashed a hand across his eyes.

"I'm so tired," he said. "I'm so tired I can't even try any more. Eth's too far away for my voice to reach her or my mind to follow, and if I tug on the cord it will snap and again she'll die. I daren't do that, Nemony. I just daren't. And I can't think of anything else."

He covered his face and wept and Nemony put her arms round him. His grief became hers and she wanted to cry too. Eth was dear to them both and all day she had been searching the auric plane around Arbroth and found no trace of her. Small wonder if, as Cable said, her dream-body had left its orbit. And Mistress Agla, in the grip of her own exhaustion, slept in the rocking chair and was no longer aware. She, too, had done her best, and her powers were greater than Nemony's. She had ranged through the higher planes, spoken with spirits and learned nothing at all – except that Eth was not among them.

"Wherever she is," murmured Nemony, "it's through no fault of yours or mine, Cable."

"But I feel so useless," sobbed Cable.

"We've done everything we can," Nemony assured him.

Cable sniffed. "But all that we've done is not enough, is it? And I was her acolyte, Nemony, but I failed to do my job! I stopped being vigilant and let her escape me. I could have made it to Malroth, maybe, if she had been there, but she's light-years away, out among the stars. I know she's there and I want to help her but I'm just not capable... I don't know how..."

"It's a rare ability," an old voice murmured, "but I know someone who can follow anyone anywhere, providing they are alive."

Cable and Nemony turned their heads. Hope rose in both of them, and a strange vermilion light gleamed in Mistress Agla's eyes as she heaved herself from the rocking chair.

"Go and ask Brenner to serve supper," she told Cable. "I'll eat first, then return by trans-matt to the Academy. It may take a few days for my message to reach the person in question and a few days more before he gets here – it depends where he is and how hard it is to find him – but find him I will. You, meanwhile, will keep the girl's body alive – feed her milk and soup and honey water – tube it down her throat if you have to, but keep her alive! I shall be back before long, in any case, to judge at her brother's trial."

*

Eth had regained enough energy to translate herself back to the auric plane. Through metal walls, gone insubstantial as mist, she entered the ship. Its fabric was grey all around her, yet the great vault glowed with uncountable human auras, bright aureoles of colour round each sleeping figure. Seen from that dimension they were indistinguishable from the inhabitants of Arbroth and not alien at all, yet when she paused to study them she became less certain of that. Their auras were marred. Each one, to a greater or lesser extent, displayed the evidence of psychic corruption, black filaments streaming like smoke from their sleeping minds. Awakened, they would be as Liadd – twisted, irrational and dangerous to know – and their collective presence filled her with dismay.

And was he like the rest of them? she wondered. The boy with blue eyes she had returned here to find? Would he, too, attempt to destroy her as Liadd had done? His aura flickered, blue as Cable's, moving along the far end of the gantry and too far away for her to tell. Torn between curiosity and concern for her own safety, Eth hesitated a moment before she followed.

CHAPTER ELEVEN

Troy felt strange at first. He was confused and his heartbeat was very erratic. His breathing was laboured, his eyes slow to focus, and his limbs shaky and weak. If not for Jack Wynn-Stanley's supporting arm, he would have been unable to walk at all. In the ship's medical quarters, Troy underwent a series of supervised exercises from mental arithmetic, flexing his fingers, wiggling his toes and focusing on an eye-chart, to knee-bends and press-ups and running on the spot. Then, after a light meal in the staff lounge, he felt better, restored to himself, human and functioning again – but not for long.

Half a dozen crew members gathered for an evening meal and a few hours of leisure before they began their shift. Men and women, whose names Troy failed to remember, sought to include him in their conversations. The room seemed suddenly overcrowded. Chattering voices plied him with personal questions, or else made reference to four years of Earth's history that he knew nothing about. Then someone switched on the music, but the abrasive sound added to his mental confusion. The video screen flickered with scenes from some old film, warm air hissed through the air-conditioning grilles and striplights in the ceiling flashed and buzzed. He was surrounded by noise and movement and reflected brightness, light glinting on the bar optics and the chrome fitments of the food vendor, on the glass-topped coffee tables and the silver vinyl armchairs, walls and floors and automatic doors. At the far end of the room, pool-balls clashed on the green baize table. Everything seemed harsh and surreal, jarring his nerves and bombarding his senses, an overload of external stimuli he felt unable to deal with.

Troy had been sleeping for the past four years, but after couple of hours awake all he wanted was dim light, and quietness, and somewhere to escape to where he could sleep again. He headed for the door that led to the crew quarters, just cubby-hole cabins, one of which would be assigned to him. It was a few minutes after twenty-two hundred hours, according to the clock on the wall, and time aboard the ship kept to a strictly circadian rhythm. The members of each skeleton crew were expected to serve a twelve-hour shift throughout their six months on duty, but Troy had already been informed by Dr Wynn-Stanley that he was not officially due on duty until the following day. He studied the duty roster on the notice-board for the number of his cabin, and went on to read the names of those who shared his shift. There was one qualified medic who was Dr Wynn-Stanley; one junior bio-technician who was himself; one senior computer operator who was his father; one senior engineer; one junior mechanic and one systems operator. Six people and a Flight Officer: J. Verity Morrison, Troy's mother.

Altogether, it was a nice cosy family reunion, and for a moment Troy was tempted to head for the bridge and search them out. Four years of separation could make for an interesting resumption of the relationship with his parents. But maybe he had better take a shower first? Wake himself up, and calm himself down, and return to the staff lounge when they came off duty?

The door to the crew quarters opened before him and shut behind him, sealing him into a bliss of silence and shadowy blue light. In front of him was a long empty corridor with closed doors on one side and round portholes on the other. He paused to watch the stars flash past, curved yellow streaks against the black background of space. And when he continued on his way, the corridor was no longer empty.

Halfway along, someone stood at the intersection as if they were uncertain of which way to go. At that distance Troy could not see her clearly, just the sapphire blue of her dress and an indigo sheen of light on her long dark hair. She was another off-duty crew member, he supposed. Or maybe not. A frail green luminescence shimmered round her and as he drew nearer, and she turned to regard him, Troy went rigid with shock.

The girl was older than he remembered and no longer a child. The thrust of her breasts and the curves of her body beneath the clinging blue shift assured him of that. She was taller, too, and had lost her gawkiness – her dusky limbs were fleshed with a woman's grace. But it was her eyes he remembered most of all, brilliant tangerine eyes, recognising him just as he recognised her. She hesitated for a moment, stared at him intently. Then, as if she had made up her mind on something, he saw the sudden flash of her smile, the impetus of greeting that caused her move towards him.

He stayed where he was, incapable of movement, his heartbeat hammering, his eyes drinking in the sight of her. He noticed that she did not walk but drifted and, vaguely, through her body, he could see the doors and walls. But she was no hallucination and never had been. She was a ghost, perhaps? The disincarnate form of someone dead? His voice was a dry whisper as she approached.

"Who are you? And what do you want?"

A blast of blackness zoomed through his head, and a feeling of longing gripped his guts, but the girl spoke in an alien language and her name, Eth, was all he could understand. Or it might have been the generic term for female? Troy did not know. He simply looked for an alarm bell, then noticed the number on the cabin door and changed his mind. Cabin 17 was his for a while, private and free from intrusion. And what possible threat could a ghost-girl pose to the security of the ship?

"You'd better come in," he said.

The cabin was soundproofed and as small as a cupboard. There was a wardrobe, a desk with a computer console, a swivel chair and a bed. Eth sat cross-legged on the end of it, her green aura clearer now against the bare white wall behind her, her orange eyes shining in the soft yellow light. And it was weird how she managed to communicate. She seemed to shove an image directly into Troy's mind, name it in her own language, then wait for him to name it in his. But she was quicker than he was and better at remembering. Her rapid grasp of English was almost uncanny. She learned to string words together into quite complex sentences, whereas he, in her language, struggled to recall the first simple words she had taught him.

Finally Eth shook her head.

"I learn... you don't learn," she announced.

"Sorry," said Troy.

She pointed to the centre of her brow. "We had better talk in pictures," she said.

It might have been the cryogenic effects on his brain that slowed him but he stared at her, uncomprehendingly, not knowing what she meant. Take things easy, Dr Wynn-Stanley had said, but already Troy had worked that night as he had never worked before, and still he failed to understand her, what she was and how she came to be there.

"I send and you mind read," Eth went on.

"I don't know how," he told her.

"Close your eyes and try not to think," she instructed.

He did as she bade and the images filled his head, dream-like visions of a green–brown world, a planet of lakes and forests and mountains. It was called Arbroth, Eth told him, and it seemed strangely familiar, yet the moment he began to wonder why, the images fled and his mind became a blank.

"Try not to think," Eth repeated.

Troy did not find it easy to maintain a state of mental receptivity. As a telepathic subject, he was close to useless. He saw in snatches, between thought and thought, glimpses of the planet's landscape and the orange orb of its moon that Eth called Malroth, a sun she called the Roth Star. And there were glimpses of the village where she lived, nestling at the foot of the mountains and a large black pyramid in the central square and squat stone houses built around it. Native people, dusky-skinned as she was, went about their daily business – simple people, men herding a flock of goat-like animals, fishermen and craftsmen, girls churning cheese in a dairy, a plump wife kneading dough. He had a feeling of peace and deep contentment, a sense of timelessness, of a way of life bound to the land that sustained it yet boundless in its meaning. But invariably he interrupted, his thoughts racing ahead towards a conclusion.

"It's nice," he said. "A non-technological society. I like it… but I don't understand. Everything you've shown me of Arbroth suggests it's a substantial world and so are its inhabitants. But you don't have that same solidity, Eth. So what are you? Some kind of ghost? And how did you get here?"

Her orange eyes looked puzzled.

"Ghost? Solidity? Substantial? Non-technological? I don't understand those words. Think me their pictures, Troy."

Words were symbols. Troy had used them readily from the age of two, yet he was totally unpractised at conceiving the appropriate mental images. Raised in the twenty-second century, his imagination had never been fostered. The images of things had always been there, already formed and in front of him, on the inescapable video screens used for both leisure and learning. Now he had to struggle to utilise an unfamiliar part of his mind, grapple with an ability stymied from birth.

Briefly, after long minutes of trying and failing and resorting partly to recall, Troy succeeded. He remembered the death of his grandfather on board the space-station, the funeral ceremony and his imaginary ghost rising from his body before it was committed to the recycling unit.

Eth smiled in response. "I am not dead, Troy. This is my dream-body."

Gradually, though a series of mind-pictures interspersed with words, Eth went on to explain, and Troy's only problem then was in believing her. She claimed to be able to step from her physical body at will and travel through alternative dimensions of reality that his rational mind denied the existence of. She claimed her flesh and blood counterpart was left behind on Arbroth and she had been blasted into space by a psychic encounter with her brother that had rendered her unconscious. She had woken to find herself adrift, not knowing where she was and too badly damaged to find her way home. Then she had seen the space ship, she said, a big metal beetle flying between the stars. She had peered through a window of the cryogenic chamber and witnessed Troy, whom she thought to be dead, come back to life.

"So how did you get inside?" asked Troy.

"I passed through the wall," Eth replied.

"Now pull the other one," said Troy.

"Pull the other what?" asked Eth.

Troy sighed.

Her tangerine eyes were fixed on his face, as if she would drag the meaning from his mind. And when he finally reported her presence, as eventually he would have to, his mother would never buy an explanation like that. It may be theoretically possible to walk through walls, pass through the spaces between the atoms of which all substance was composed, but it had never been proved.

"You have to be joking," he said.

She understood immediately.

And before he could blink, she was gone.

Troy gaped at the space on the bed where Eth had been sitting. And a moment later she reappeared, stepped through the solid fabric of the wall, only to fade before his eyes and vanish again. And into his mind, stunned out of thought, came an image of the room as she was seeing it – a vague grey surround, ghostly sheen on ghostly furniture, the glowing white oval of the wall light and himself sitting on the swivel chair, his body colourless and indistinct, an electric blue aura shimmering around him.

Troy stared at his aura in complete fascination. It was far more beautiful than ever he could have visualised, but it was also marred. Wisps of darkness, like tongues of black fire, emanated from the shadow shape of his torso and skull.

"Ill thoughts damage you," murmured the unseen Eth. "Give rise to bad emotions and unstable behaviour. And they were the same, all those frozen people who slept with you – only worse, much worse – many of them mad and sick as Liadd, and just as dangerous."

The room returned to normal as she re-materialised on the end of Troy's bed, leaned against the now solid wall and closed her eyes. And he may have been imagining, but there was a dimness about

133

her, as if the translation she had made to that other dimension had drained something from her. Her voice sounded weary and sad.

"There is too much bad energy here and nothing to sustain me. And how will I get home, Troy? My body will die if I don't rejoin it, and so will I."

He gazed at her anxiously, not knowing how to help her or what to do. And her diagnosis troubled him, too close to the truth for him to dismiss it. If he were honest, he was bound to admit that now and then he *was* plagued by ill thoughts and bad emotions. And if ever he failed to keep a grip on himself, he would indeed be prone to uncertain behaviour. And yes, everyone from Earth was similar or worse. The three thousand people sleeping on board this ship would one day awake to despoil another world. Another world seen in a virtual reality video – green and brown with lakes and forests and mountains, herds of goat-like creatures and dusky native people with orange eyes. Suddenly Troy knew why Arbroth had seemed familiar. It was the world to which they were heading. And did Eth know, too?

"Why are you here?" he demanded.

"I've already told you," she murmured.

"But why come here?" Troy insisted. "Why come here and not somewhere else? Three times now you and I have met. Is it a coincidence?"

Eth opened her eyes, and he saw the comprehension dawn within them.

"On Arbroth we don't believe in coincidence," she said.

"Then why are you here?" he repeated.

"Why are you?" she said.

Troy might have told her then, but the buzzer sounded for the start of his shift and, over the intercom, his mother's voice ordered him to report to the bridge. He had neither slept nor rested, but J. Verity Morrison was the Flight Officer in charge and automatically he rose to obey, then paused by the door to look back.

"Will you stay here until I return?" he asked.

Eth inclined her head.

"I have nowhere else to go," she said simply.

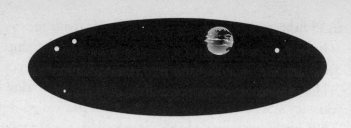

CHAPTER TWELVE

At the speed of light *Exodus* 27 cut across the galaxy, yet Troy had no sensation of movement until he entered the bridge. There, on the high gantry, the huge surrounding windows gave a different impression. Wings of colour battered his eyes as the ship hurtled through a curving corridor of stars towards a whirlpool of darkness. Troy clutched the handrail, swallowed back an upsurge of nausea, and headed down the steps to the flight deck. Under the striplights, with a solider floor beneath his feet and blank walls round him, his sickness lessened and he wound his way among navigational computers towards the central dais where his parents were sitting.

Neither noticed Troy's arrival. Their attention was fixed on the vast electronic star-chart beyond them. On it, a tiny blinking light showed the ship's whereabouts, almost midway between Earth and Croxley's Star, or the Roth Star as Eth had called it. Then his father touched the computer keys and their trajectory was superimposed in a fine line of laser light on the black background.

"We definitely need to correct our course," he said.

"Can you handle the calculations?" asked Verity.

"I am a qualified operator," Troy's father replied.

"Who, along with the rest of us, has never been put to the test," said Verity. "When it comes to deep space you're as much a greenhorn as I am, Bill."

Troy's father shrugged.

"No company who wants to stay in business would send seasoned crew on a one-way trip, Verity. We're all we've got. And I'm all *you've* got. So do I make the correction or not? It's your decision."

Verity frowned.

"I could ignore it, I suppose. Postpone making a decision all together and leave it to my successor."

"You're the Flight Officer in charge, sweetheart."

"What would you do if you were me?"

"You could use Hargreaves to double-check," Troy's father suggested.

Troy coughed to announce his presence and his

parents swung to face him. Their familiar eyes regarded him, his mother's blue and identical to his own, his father's brown and unfathomable, soft as his voice.

"You're looking rough, son."

"And just because the Flight Officer in charge happens to be your mother doesn't mean you can turn up on duty looking like a slob!" said Verity. "You might at least have shaved and combed your hair!"

"Sorry," said Troy.

"And where were you last night?" asked his father.

"We waited in the lounge for ages," said Verity. "What was so important that you couldn't even come and say hello?"

"Sorry," Troy said again.

"Let's hear it then," said his father.

"Let's hear what?" asked Troy.

"Your explanation," said Verity.

Troy hesitated, then glanced at the star-chart on the wall.

"Is that where we are? Over halfway? It's amazing, isn't it? We've come all that distance and I never knew a thing. How long have you two been on duty?"

"Since yesterday morning," said Verity. "And don't change the subject! If you were feeling groggy, then say so and I'll understand. But right now, the way we see it, we have been deliberately ignored by our own offspring – and that's a different matter! If you don't wish to associate with us, by all means return to your cryogenic berth and I'll resuscitate someone else in your place."

"It's not like that," said Troy.

"So where were you then?"

"And what are you hiding?" asked his father.

Troy chewed his lip. She was beautiful and fascinating, the dream-body of a girl from an alien culture. And sooner or later he would have to tell them. So it may as well be now.

"There's an alien girl in my cabin," he said.

There was a moment of silence.

The computers hummed.

And the stars flashed overhead.

"Good one," said his father. "And is it she of the orange eyes and dusky skin whom you saw on board the space-station?"

"Yes," said Troy. "Only she's four years older than she was then. Her name's Eth and she comes from a planet named Arbroth – which is where we happen to be going."

"Arbroth," said his father. "That's a nice name for a world. And what's a girl from Arbroth doing in your cabin?"

Troy told most of what he knew – how Eth had been involved in some kind of psychic battle with her brother that had drained her of energy and blasted her into space. She was lost, said Troy, and separated from herself, her physical body left behind on the planet and her ghost-body stranded aboard the ship.

His father laughed.

"Go and take a cold shower, son."

"Or consult Dr Wynn-Stanley," said his mother.

"Meaning you don't believe me?" asked Troy.

"Sorry," said Verity.

"So go and see for yourself," said Troy.

"Pack it in!" Verity said crossly.

"It's his age," said his father. "It was funny to begin with, son, but you're taking it too far."

Troy felt narked enough to retaliate.

"Listen, Pater! I'll tell you again, just one more time: there's an alien girl in my cabin! I'm not joking. Not hallucinating. Not projecting! She's there! Right? Disembodied but as real as the rest of us! And that's the truth!"

His father believed him then.

And so did his mother.

He saw a look on her face of sheer dismay.

"God Almighty!" groaned Verity.

Verity sounded the alarm before Troy could stop her

and both crews, night shift as well as day shift, were gathered in the corridor when Troy opened the cabin door. He half-expected to find Eth gone, himself the butt of his mother's anger and his sanity under question, but she slept on his bed, curled like a foetus, her green aura shimmering round her and the white coverlet visible through the blue of her shift.

Unceremoniously, Verity elbowed him aside and Jack Wynn-Stanley followed her, medic and Flight Officer in their respective uniforms, bending to examine the alien intruder.

"Can we wake her?" asked Verity.

"I'd be inclined to let her sleep," Dr Wynn-Stanley replied. "If what Troy says is true, and she has been through some grave psychological ordeal, then she obviously needs time to recover."

"She can hardly stay here!" retorted Verity.

Troy edged his way inside the cabin. "Why not?" he demanded.

"She's alien, for God's sake!"

"She's not doing any harm!" said Troy.

"Until she recovers maybe!"

"She's just a girl..."

"As Flight Officer in charge...!"

"Jump down, Mother!"

"Don't you speak to me—"

"Cool it, son," his father said from the doorway.

"We could move her to Medical," Dr Wynn-Stanley suggested.

"Why bother?" asked Verity. "There are rules regarding alien life forms encountered in deep space. We avoid them! Right? So I want her off this ship at the first opportunity!"

"You can hardly evict someone made of thin air!" said Troy. "And Eth's as human as we are, Mum. Put her back on Arbroth in her physical body and you wouldn't think twice about hiring her as a domestic servant when we actually land!"

"She'd be lovely to look at, too," murmured his father.

Verity turned on him. "That's just the kind of remark I would expect from a man! Why can't you say something useful, Bill? Give me some constructive advice as to what I ought to do?"

"You don't need me to tell you what to do, sweetheart."

"But we're all involved in this…"

"And unfortunately you bear the responsibility, Verity," said Dr. Wynn-Stanley. "Now why don't we go elsewhere and discuss it?"

For a moment longer Verity lingered, gazing down at the girl on Troy's bed. Such an occurrence was without precedent in the history of galactic exploration and the significance appalled her. Native populations abounded throughout the charted regions of the Milky Way but there had never been any evidence of a culture intellectually advanced enough for inter-stellar travel. The girl might be a non-physical apparition but she was hardly alone in her abilities. Whatever planet she came from – and she was certainly reminiscent of the sample population Verity had seen on the virtual reality video of the world around Croxley's Star – there would be others who shared her talents. And if she had been involved in a psychic battle, as Troy claimed she had, then they were likely to be hostile. That meant, to Verity's way of thinking, there was not only a distinct possibility of an unfriendly welcome awaiting them on the planet but also an equal possibility the ship could be invaded as well. Three years in the future any alterations in their landing plans could wait on a general consultation with the senior crew but, as Flight Officer in charge of the ship, her immediate priority was to ensure its safety.

Determinedly, she straightened her back, pulled down the cuffs of her scarlet uniform and strode into the corridor. A dozen crew awaited her decision – and she was tempted to order a resuscitation of all the crew members held in cryogenic suspension and her fellow Flight Officers as well – yet she resisted. One alien presence, passive and sleeping, whose hostility was not yet proven, hardly warranted a full-scale red alert. Verity nodded to a junior mechanic.

"Go and get a stun-gun from the armoury, Lewis, and stand guard in the doorway. I want to know the minute that girl awakens. If nothing's changed within four hours, I'll send Hargreaves to relieve you. And don't shoot unless you have to."

"There's no need to go to those lengths," said Troy. Verity ignored him.

"On your way, Lewis." The youth in green uniform saluted and, before his footsteps faded, Verity continued with her precautions. "Take over the bridge, Hargreaves. Switch on the main scanners and maintain a constant watch on the surrounding space, and use the infra-red frequencies as well. You go with him, Nancy. I want all internal videos running and on screen, including those in the cryogenic chamber and the cargo holds. I'll join you as and when."

"For crying out loud!" Troy objected. "We're not expecting a blasted invasion, are we?"

But again Verity ignored him. Hargreaves and Nancy obeyed.

"Those of you not on duty return to your cabins and get some sleep," Verity said briskly. "Should you hear the alarm bell then make your way to the bridge, or use your initiative."

The remaining crew members nodded and departed.

"What the hell are you doing?" asked Troy.

And still Verity ignored him.

"I want an in-depth discussion of this situation," she said to Jack Wynn-Stanley. "Go ahead to the staff lounge and I'll join you in a minute. You, too, Bill," she told Troy's father. "And get me a coffee – hot, black and strong as the machine will make it."

"Will do," Troy's father replied. "And go easy, Verity."

The two men left and finally Verity paid heed to Troy. Her cheeks were flushed, and blue anger blazed in her eyes.

"If you ever question or undermine my orders again in front of anyone I'll have you slammed in the cargo hold for the next three years! Do I make myself clear?"

"But you don't understand," said Troy.

"DO I MAKE MYSELF CLEAR?" Verity repeated.

"Yes," said Troy.

"Then from now on remember it!"

She headed along the corridor to the staff lounge. Troy followed.

"You've got it all wrong, Mum! You're making a crisis out of nothing! Eth's no threat. She needs help, for Christ's sake! And what's the point in setting a guard on someone who can walk through walls?"

The automatic door opened before them. Verity turned to regard him.

"So she can do that, can she? And what else can she do? Blow the electrical circuits? Switch off the cryogenics? Bug the computers? Sabotage the main drive units?"

"Don't be ridiculous!" said Troy.

Verity's voice was venomous. "I'm doing my job, that's all!"

The silver vinyl armchair sighed beneath her weight as she thumped herself down. Striplights flickered and the vending machine hissed and spat black liquid into plastic cups. And despite the presence of his father and Dr Wynn-Stanley, Troy was not about to give up.

"Why won't you listen?" he asked.

"Why won't *you*?" asked Verity. "You're talking about energy – psycho-kinetic energy! Power enough to blast that girl light-years across the universe! That's not spoon-bending, Troy! And if she herself isn't dangerous then the one who did it to her is, and there could be a whole race of them on their way here! I would be an incompetent fool if I didn't take precautions!"

"Your mother's right," said Dr Wynn-Stanley.

Troy frowned and took a seat beside her. "But if Eth's representative of her kind…"

"We don't know that," said Dr Wynn-Stanley.

"And it's hardly likely," said his father. "She's female, Troy. Or hadn't you noticed? The males of the humanoid species are usually far more aggressive." Gently, he placed the full cups of coffee on the table.

"You're not aggressive!" Troy said hotly.

"We're talking of generalities, son."

"And you're an aberration, are you?"

"I like to think I'm intelligent enough to control—"

"So maybe they are on Arbroth, too!"

"After what you've told us, Troy, it's highly improbable," Dr Wynn-Stanley commented. "On your own admission the girl was attacked…"

"And that was the aberration," Troy insisted. "If you'd talked to Eth as I have, if you'd had glimpses of the world she lives in and the culture that raised her, you'd know they weren't given to violence. And it's a non-technological society anyway! So what possible—?"

"I deal in facts, not fantasies!" interrupted Verity. "Try and be rational, Troy, just for the duration of this conversation. And consider the odds against a pacifist population. It's only in the last couple of hundred years on Earth that we've made any attempt to combat our own warlike tendencies, and still violence is rampant in our society. And we're an advanced civilisation, for Christ's sake! So don't try telling me that some backward planet with a primitive population has discovered the secret of harmonious existence, because I won't believe you!"

Troy rose to his feet. "It's you who's not being rational, Mother! It's bad enough transporting all the crap from Earth to pollute other planets, but you don't have to credit everyone in the universe with the same idiotic tendencies as ourselves! They might have got it right on Arbroth! And before you pass judgement on Eth, try holding a trial! Most common criminals get that much justice – even from stinkers like us!"

The door closed behind him as he left the room, and Verity sighed. "Is he going crazy? Or am I?"

"I'd say he was emotionally involved," murmured Jack Wynn-Stanley.

"What are we going to do?" asked Bill.

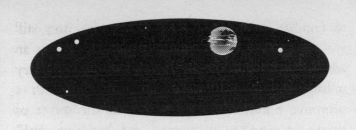

CHAPTER THIRTEEN

Verity stood in the doorway. It was an hour before the day shift reported for duty. Troy not yet risen and the rest of the crew were taking breakfast in the lounge. And for once the medical department was empty, except for Jack Wynn-Stanley and herself – and the girl curled on the cot.

"Is there any change?" she asked.

The medic shook his head. Dark circles ringed his eyes and his white coat was crumpled, as if he had slept in it, or else not slept at all. There was no change, he said wearily, and Troy was right in his observations. The girl *was* fading.

Verity sighed and approached the glass partition to view the bed on which Eth lay. It had been four days since Troy and his father had carried her there, a weightless burden on a white counterpane to be deposited in the small isolation ward under the medic's care. And for four days Eth had remained sleeping, a sleep so deep no one could rouse her, a comatose ghost in an oxygen tent, her apple-green aura flickering around her.

Apart from the evidence of their own eyes, only the heat-sensitive scanning equipment confirmed she existed, a pattern of psychedelic colours on a video screen. There was no way of checking her pulse, if she had one, of taking her temperature or making a white cell count. No way of establishing what ailed her. Impossible to attach to her insubstantial body the electrodes that would monitor her essential life processes, or the machines that would sustain her. And as a medic trained in the mechanics of flesh and blood reality, Jack Wynn-Stanley was unable to revive her.

"Is there nothing you can do?" asked Verity.

"I could try praying," the medic replied.

Verity glanced at him.

Attitudes had changed towards Eth since the initial panic faded and the feared invasion failed to materialise. Members of the crew, placed on alert status, gradually relaxed their guard. Their anxiety for their own lives shifted to an anxiety for hers.

Her presence concerned them, and the tales Troy told invoked their sympathy. She was young and pretty and they wanted her to recover, wanted to meet her and question her, get to know her as Troy had done. Even Verity wanted that much. But still Eth slept and Troy remained the only source of information they had on her, the only source understanding.

This was her dream-body, he had said, a psychic counterpart of the physical body she had left behind on Arbroth, the as yet unconfirmed planet to which the ship was heading. Such an exact replica, Verity noted, every minute detail of a physical being perfectly reproduced, from the veins in her arms and the half moons of her fingernails, to the dark of her eyelashes and the black drifts of her hair, from the stitchery on her leather sandals to the delicate seams on the blue linen shift she was wearing. There was nothing nebulous or indistinct about her, although she was transparent. But her physical body would die if she did not get back to it, Troy had said. And now Jack Wynn-Stanley agreed that her image on board the ship was also fading.

"I see no difference in her," said Verity.

"There's a growing predominance of cool colours on the video-screen," the medic replied. "Which means the scanner is registering a substantial heat loss. And her aura is dimmer than it was."

"Are you sure about that?"

"If you compare the spectrograph readings..."

"So are you saying this dream-body of hers is also dying?"

"It depends what you mean by death," murmured Dr Wynn-Stanley.

Verity frowned and seated herself in the consulting chair. She had always believed that death was an ending, a cessation of life, but the reality of Eth caused her to reconsider. It was possible that all people were as she was, insubstantial beings trapped in the temporary shell of a physical body, immortal entities released at death into some other dimension. The concept was not so unusual. It had its adherents on Earth, even in Western culture, but Verity had not been among them.

"I never did go in for all this New Age stuff," she said.

"You and me neither," said Dr Wynn-Stanley. "Yet what other explanation is there? She's dying to this dimension maybe, but, seemingly, that doesn't preclude her continued existence elsewhere. According to Troy she was able to walk through solid walls – vanish from the end of his bed and reappear..."

"According to Troy!" Verity said brusquely.

"I don't think he made it up," said the medic.

"Maybe not," said Verity. "But he's made it personal, Jack. Bad energy aboard this ship and nothing to sustain her, that's what he claims. According to him we're all mad, sick and dangerous – and I can't handle the implications of that. I can't handle him or what this girl means. There are too many questions, Jack. Too many issues involved. It's beyond the scope of my job…"

Jack Wynn-Stanley shrugged unsympathetically.

"Don't worry, Verity. The girl will be gone in another day or so. End of problem for all of us."

Verity stared at the eye-chart on the wall. "But Troy won't be gone," she said, her voice sounding bitter. "And I may have wanted her off this ship, but not in that way, Jack! The questions will remain. Is it definitely her world we are going to? And if it is, then what kind of culture awaits us that the survey ship reported as 'primitive'? There are three thousand people destined to land on that planet. Their safe passage is my responsibility. But what about their safety *after* we land? I need answers, Jack, that only this girl can give me. Surely there must be something you can do! There must be some way you can prevent her from fading, or dying, or whatever it is, some way to reverse the process and restore her to consciousness."

Jack Wynn-Stanley paced the floor, his shoes squeaking on the linoleum.

"If there is," he said, "then I don't know it. I was trained under the auspices of the British Medical Association, remember? Blood, flesh and bone, Verity, is what I am qualified to treat! Not some ethereal form that's supposed not to exist! What the girl needs is a dose of psychic energy, an alternative healer, maybe, someone who uses crystals or colour therapy or chakra manipulation."

"What's that?" asked Verity.

"The kind of hocus-pocus you and I prefer not to believe in! You have the passenger list. Is there anyone like that on board? No, of course there isn't! Just three thousand materialistic, spiritually bereft individuals who haven't got a clue – and that's including you and me!"

Verity stared at him. His powerlessness made him angry and light winked on his spectacles, winked on the stethoscope that hung uselessly around his neck. Verity understood. The girl from Arbroth challenged him, too, stripped him of his former beliefs and overturned his concepts of reality. He, too, was confronted by questions that had no answers, issues beyond the scope of his job – the medic in conflict with the man. Verity rose to her feet.

"You're beginning to sound like Troy!" she complained.

"What's that meant to mean?" Troy asked from the doorway.

"Excuse me," said Verity. "I have a ship to run."

Troy stared through the clear plastic of the oxygen tent. His voice was wild. "We can't just sit here, for Christ's sake!"

Angrily, the medic responded. "I've already been through all this with your mother!"

"What does she care?"

"More than you think!" retorted Dr Wynn-Stanley.

Helplessly they regarded Eth. Troy's voice could not wake her – he had tried that several times over the last few days. And gradually her green aura faded and her image grew more and more ghost-like. Bad energy and nothing to sustain her, she had said. So what did she need? he thought desperately. Food and water were physical needs, so what did a dream-body need? What was good energy? What exactly was it that Eth lacked?

"Man cannot live by bread alone," muttered Troy.

"Pardon?" said Dr Wynn-Stanley.

"Someone said that once," said Troy.

"It's in the Bible," said Dr Wynn-Stanley.

"But what does it mean?"

"I'm hardly a theologian, Troy."

"You mean you don't believe something exists unless you can examine it through a microscope?"

"That's not what I said."

"No," said Troy. "You can't, can you? Because it's obvious she exists. And what is she? Not physical. The ghost from the machine, maybe, if we think of our bodies as machines. And are we like her? Do we all have a dream-body within us? If so, what do we feed it on? What do we mean by food for the soul, Dr Wynn-Stanley?"

"That's a very hypothetical question, Troy."

"Then give me a hypothetical answer."

"You're thinking about spiritual nourishment, are you?"

"Yes," said Troy.

"Then surely that must vary with the individual?"

"But what is it we need other than bread and circuses?"

Dr Wynn-Stanley sighed and shook his head.

"Beauty?" he said tentatively. "Poetry or music? High mountains? Waterfalls? Deserts? Any kind of natural landscape maybe? Anything that inspires and uplifts. Cuckoos and rainbows? Birdsong and butterflies' wings? Whatever turns you on, I suppose."

"Whatever turns you on," said Troy. "Not necessarily sexual – but it's some kind of relationship, isn't it?

Suddenly Troy knew, and it was nothing to do with beauty or attraction, the male–female thing, poetry or passion. Before Dr Wynn-Stanley could stop him, he unfastened the oxygen tent and stepped inside.

"What the hell do you think you're doing?" the medic demanded.

"Turn it off," said Troy.

"Since when have you been in charge of this department?"

"She doesn't need oxygen."

"I'm thinking of the contamination factors!"

"Take that up with my mother," said Troy. "There are three thousand contaminating factors on their way to Arbroth, so she may as well get used to me."

"Get out of there, Troy!"

"Just give me ten minutes, Doctor."

"Ten minutes to do what?"

Troy shook his head. He did not know yet and could not explain. He merely sensed that he was the only chance Eth had.

"Please?" he said. "It's worth a try, isn't it? If someone's dying, anything's worth a try."

Jack Wynn-Stanley shrugged and turned on his heel, strode into the outer office and closed the intervening door. Seated on the bed beside Eth, Troy could still see him through the glass partition seated at the computer console, tight-lipped and pointedly ignoring him. Then he focused his attention on the girl from Arbroth. Somehow or other he had to feed her and nourish her, share his strength and his energy. He had to give of the love in him and the life in him, rekindle her connection to all that existed in this dimension, call her back into being before she faded away.

"Eth?"

He lay beside her, reached out to touch. He had to forget about his physical body – she was as intangible as air to his flesh-and-blood hand. He had to reach for her in some other way. Weak as he was at visualisation, he again resorted to memory, recalling himself as Eth had seen him from that other dimension, the flaring blue of his aura merging with hers as he moved nearer.

"Eth?"

She seemed not to hear, not to respond. He spoke to her again but she was gone beyond words and he had to find some other way to reach her, deeper than words or thoughts or even images. He had to forget about his mind and all he thought he was and simply be.

His ghost fingers felt the strands of her hair, traced the shape of her, a tingle of warmth, an existence next to his own. What powered his life could pass directly into her. She had no resistance and it would be easy to impose on her, bend her to his will, but that was not what he wanted. He just wanted to share with her a portion of the energy he possessed and she needed, because he cared.

"Do you hear me, Eth? This is all I have, all I can give you. Take it. Take it... Do you hear me?"

His ghost lips touched her lips and, just for a moment, Troy loved. He felt the energy flow through the link between them, felt himself give of some vital force and felt her stir.

"Get out of there, Troy! Now this minute!"

The voice intruded, like an alarm clock blasting him from a dream. The link with Eth was broken and Troy sat up, suddenly returned to a sense of his own separateness. Pain seared through his head and his body felt tight as a carapace that no longer fitted. And there was a look on Dr Wynn-Stanley's face that Troy had never seen before, a mixture of rage and disgust.

"Out!" the medic repeated.

"But I hadn't finished!" Troy objected.

"So go and take a cold shower!"

His father's words – and suddenly Troy understood.

Shocked and angry, he stared at the medic.

And on the bed behind him, Eth opened her eyes.

CHAPTER FOURTEEN

Nervously, Eth regarded them: people as gaudy as flowers in their brightly coloured clothes, alien people with pale skins and pale faces, with hair brown as puddle water or yellow as straw – a woman whose eyes were dark and slanted and whose hair was as black as Eth's own, a brown-skinned man with brown eyes, and the man in a white coat who had been there when she awakened, impassive now after his quarrel with Troy. The people stared at her and smiled at her, made pointed comments, asked Troy and the other man questions about her as if she were incapable of answering for herself, incapable of understanding. Everyone appeared to be friendly but Eth could sense their underlying uncertainty, the emotions that simmered below the surface.

Her nervousness grew and Troy was the only one she knew, standing triumphant in the midst of them, his blue eyes laughing now his venom was spent. She did not know what had caused his fit of rage or what had happened between himself and her, but something had, and she was awake because of it, alive because of it, her energy suddenly restored. It was as if he had touched her at some deep level and become linked to her very soul. She could feel the connection just as surely as she felt it with Cable – irretractable, unbreakable, another being who would care for her for always, in spite of what he was.

"Troy?"

He turned his head.

"Who are these people? And what do they want?"

She was introduced to them then: John Lewis; Nancy Kwang; Ellis Hargreaves; Jack Wynn-Stanley, the medic, who had watched over her; and Troy's parents, Bill and Verity Morrison. She repeated their names in a ceremony of greeting where the words they spoke had nothing to do with the feelings they felt. All the curiosity and suspicion they had shown a few moments before remained unexpressed. She wondered why they did not ask her directly but, one by one, they dispersed to their duties in other parts of the ship, until finally only

Troy and Jack Wynn-Stanley and Verity remained.

Verity was the Flight Officer in charge, the medic informed her, the person responsible for everyone else and the one who made the decisions. Solemnly Eth regarded her, a woman whom others deferred to, whose wisdom must be equal to Mistress Agla's. Her fair hair and blue eyes were similar to Troy's and her scarlet uniform was sheened with light. Relaxed and smiling, she sat on the end of Eth's bed. But again her outward appearance belied her inner uncertainty, and worry-lines creased her brow although her voice was gentle.

"Are you recovered enough to answer some questions, Eth?"

"Can't it wait?" Troy said belligerently.

Annoyance flashed in Verity's eyes, and the gentleness was gone. "Keep out of it, you!"

"She's only just emerged from a coma, for Christ's sake!"

"If she doesn't feel like it—"

"Would you if you were her?"

Verity looked to the man in the white coat. "Should I leave and come back later, Jack?"

The medic shrugged. "Troy's the expert," he said bitterly.

"So push off, both of you!" Troy said rudely.

Eth saw the woman's knuckles tighten. The skin

shone white beneath the light and her body stiffened. The medic's hand rested restrainingly on her shoulder.

"Why don't we go and grab a coffee?" he suggested. Verity relaxed slowly, her face smoothing to an accepting mask.

"A good idea," she agreed, and turned again to Eth. "I'll come and see you later, when you're rested," she said. "Or, if you feel able, perhaps you will come and see me on the bridge? It's important that I talk with you, I think."

Eth nodded and they left the room.

Heat from a wall duct hissed in the silence.

And Troy grinned.

"Sorry about that."

"Are you?" said Eth. "You don't look sorry to me, Troy."

He grinned again.

"It's called oneupmanship," he informed her.

"It's dishonest," said Eth. "Manipulating someone else to get your own way. She's your mother, and you behaved horribly."

Troy stared at her in surprise.

"I was trying to *protect* you!" he said.

"By deliberately hurting someone?" Eth frowned. "I don't want to be protected in that way, Troy. And why should I need protecting from your mother?

She didn't threaten me. All she wanted were answers to some questions."

"I stand corrected," Troy said stiffly.

"You behave towards your mother as Liadd used to behave towards mine," said Eth. "As if you despise her."

"Liadd? Your brother? The one who zapped you? I hope you're not suggesting…? Well, thanks very much, Eth! That's what I get for resuscitating you, is it? A lecture on how to show respect to my flaming parents! And so much for gratitude! Next time you can snuff it!"

It was Eth's turn to stare at him. All through their conversation she had spoken in her own language, yet he had understood it, picked up the meanings and images behind her words – a telepathic communion. And how had it happened? How had he resuscitated her and got so close to her? She saw the colour drained from his aura and sensed the resultant weariness stealing through him.

"What have you done?" she murmured.

"I don't know," he said bitterly.

Eth could imagine.

And he could interpret her sending.

"Yes," he confirmed. "Something like that."

"You shouldn't," she said. "You shouldn't give

165

from yourself."

"I did it for *you*!" he retorted.

She sighed and rose from the bed. He was so like Liadd – his character, his tetchiness, his capacity for violence. She was unable to fathom the difference between them. Yet Liadd had taken and Troy had given, and who was she to judge the true self inside him? What raged and reacted, belittled his mother and demanded gratitude from Eth, was as unreal as the facet of Hurli that had raped and beaten Arlynn. And what was true in Troy, Eth could only love and admire.

"I don't understand you," she said.

"Ditto," said Troy.

"So now will you take me to your mother?" she asked.

Bewildered, Eth stood on the flight deck. Above the level of the gantries, the galaxy flashed past in rushing streamers of colour. Around her, a simulated universe showed on the wall charts, a darkness of space and electronic stars that shifted slowly as Troy's father depressed the computer keys, then stilled into a configuration of familiar constellations.

"Do you recognise it?" asked Verity.

"Yes," said Eth.

And now she knew that the scenes they had

shown her on a small vision screen, recorded by a survey ship a decade previously, of a green–brown world of lakes and forests and mountains, had definitely been her own. She had not been sure, never having seen it from the air, and the magnified close-ups had concentrated mostly on the landscape, places she did not know and brief glimpses of people, similar to herself, whom she had never met. But the stars were unmistakable. Apart from the absence of Malroth, she might have been standing on Arbroth staring at the night sky showing that identical pattern of stars.

"It's the same," she said.

"That confirms it then," said Troy's father.

She knew what he meant.

This ship and its sleepers were heading for Arbroth.

"So we'll give you a lift," said Troy. "And you'll be home in three years. Arriving with three thousand invaders who intend to take over. How does that grab you, Eth?"

"Did you *have* to put it like that?" asked Verity.

"It's true!" said Troy.

"Not necessarily!" Verity said curtly.

"You intend to stop it, Mother?"

"Arbroth is hardly an overcrowded planet, Troy. There is room enough for us to settle there without

167

encroaching on the territories held by its native population—"

"Since when have we on Earth ever respected other people's territorial rights?" Troy asked angrily.

"If we work out a proviso before we land…"

"F. J. Guttenham will laugh in your face! And he won't be the only one, either! They're ambitious people, Mother. They won't go along with it."

"They will if they have no other choice," said Verity.

Eth glanced from one to another, not quite understanding all their vocabulary or the basis for their antagonism, but gleaning the gist of their meaning. She had felt a moment of gladness when she realised the ship would take her home, a quick upsurge of joy that she would meet Troy again in the physical dimension, that he would be coming to share her world and maybe her life. But it fled as she grasped the wider significance, the underlying intention.

Verity smiled at her reassuringly. "Troy's exaggerating," she said.

"Am I?" Troy said wrathfully.

"We're heading for a new life, son, not a ruddy war," said his father. "There's not a man or woman on board this ship who wouldn't be prepared to settle for a few acres of land and a new beginning."

Verity nodded. "I can give you my assurance on that, Eth."

She meant what she said, Eth knew that, and so had Troy's father. And Troy himself was tired, depleted of the energy he had given and Eth had received, and far too hostile to be thinking rationally. Yet Eth had seen those sleeping alien people, seen the sickness in their auras and, in spite of Verity's assurance, she was afraid of what they might do if they came to Arbroth. Then, across the room at the small display screens, she saw Ellis Hargreaves and Nancy Kwang smile at her and wave, as if they liked her, as if she were their friend. And maybe she was mistaken, thought Eth. Maybe she had misread those auras in the cryogenic chamber and was wrong to feel afraid? Comforted, she turned her attention back to Verity.

"Will you tell us something of your way of life?" Verity asked her. "From the reports of the survey ship we gather that you live in small rural communities. There are no large cities on the planet and you practise subsistence farming. Is that correct?"

"Yes," said Eth.

"Your religion is bound up with the black pyramids around which each community is built and there is no applied technology. Are we right about

169

that, too?"

Eth hesitated.

"Don't tell her!" said Troy. "Don't tell her about the human sacrifice! Nor the arsenals of mind-blasters! Nor the armies of psychic assassins! Don't tell her, Eth!"

Eth stared at him in horror. A string of hideous images filled her head, of death and war and ritual killing, aspects of a behaviour that was unknown on Arbroth. She opened her mouth to protest but suddenly no one paid heed to her. The alarm siren wailed – heads turned – Nancy Kwang leapt to her feet.

"An intruder!" she cried.

"Where?" shouted Verity.

"In the cryogenic chamber!"

"Not any more!" yelled Ellis Hargreaves. "Whoever-it-is is passing through the cabin area now! Moving fast and coming this way!"

"So who or what is it?" shouted Verity.

"Some kind of alien life form, Ma'am!"

"It's probably one of Eth's friends," said Troy. "One of the psychic assassins she's not telling us about. They leech your energy like vampires…"

"Button it!" snapped his father.

"Get Lewis on the intercom!" Verity ordered. "Tell him we need stun-guns and to get here straight away. The rest of you keep your heads down!"

Troy's father had no time to obey. The main doors blasted open but there was no one there, no one visible anyway, just a sense of power and presence. Then, slowly, someone manifested at the top of the stairs leading down from the gantry, a being in a blaze of purple light. Heedless of the alarm sound wailing around him, he calmly surveyed the scene below as if he searched for someone.

Eth felt his gaze fix on her face and she watched, unalarmed, as he drifted down the stairs towards her. She had never seen anyone with a purple aura before but she knew what it meant. Purple was the colour of wisdom, the mark of a sage or a seer, rare and wondrous. She stared at him in awe, until she recognised who he was – the thin lips, the scar on his face, the ruthless eyes.

"Vashlian!"

"I've come to take you home," he replied.

Eth barely remembered what happened next. There was movement in the room, people emerging from their hiding places, Troy and Bill and Verity. Raised voices besieged her, meaningless among the wail of sound. And other members of the crew, roused by the alarm siren, came running onto the gantry. A laser gun fired. Shafts of rattling light aimed at Vashlian's aura were deflected by the protective shield that surrounded him to strike a nearby computer. The glass screen shattered with a shower of sparks. And Vashlian responded immediately. Waves of psychic energy radiated rapidly outwards, cut the electrics and plunged the room into darkness and silence.

Darkness, where only the stars hurtled overhead and the black shapes of people froze where they stood. Silence, before their voices took over and the laser gun could seek its mark and fire again. It was just a pause of a single moment, perhaps, but it was time enough for Vashlian to act, to reach for Eth and make the translation to the auric dimension.

The ship's control room faded instantly to grey, a vague sheen of starlight on a multitude of machines, its human crew become featureless forms contained within shining auras of colour. And no, she had not been mistaken. They were all marred, all spoiled, all contaminated, and she recognised none of them except for that pale familiar blue.

Then, as Vashlian drew her through the insubstantial walls of the ship, Troy, too, was gone. But the link remained between them, the power of life he had shared with her and the debt she would always owe him, the pain of parting, the need to be with him again. And his fear followed her across the universe, fear not for himself but for her. She heard it with her auric ears... the voice of an alien boy calling her name.

Chapter Fifteen

The summer's heat was ending in a storm that had yet to break. Nemony could feel it in the air, sullen and brooding, and the mood of the weather was reflected among the people in the council hall. The great room seemed hushed and stifling, full of tension that was also about to break. Nemony was aware of it even in herself. Sweat beaded her forehead and dampened her clothes. Her impartiality was shattered and anxiety for Eth gnawed at the pit of her stomach.

Vashlian had arrived that morning in response to Mistress Agla's message, his hair braided and beaded, his black robes powdered with the red dust of Malroth. He was no acolyte and never had been, yet the old woman had seemed confident that if anyone could discover the whereabouts of Eth's dream-body and return her to herself, it was he. His psychic powers were awesome, she had claimed. But many hours had passed since Vashlian had entered a state of trance, quit his body and begun his search, and still there was no message, still neither he nor Eth had returned.

Nemony, called late to the witness stand, had nothing more to report. The prognosis remained the same and the charge against Liadd stayed unaffected. There was little chance that Eth could be restored to her physical body without being severely psychically damaged, Nemony said, and that was providing she could be restored at all. Liadd's crime was tantamount to murder and would have been murder indeed had Hurli not intervened.

With her words the evidence was complete. Mistress Agla considered her verdict, and witnesses and character witnesses sat on the benches and waited. From her seat at the council table, Nemony regarded them, half the adult population of the village gathered together, Arlynn and Kanderin among them, holding themselves apart on opposite sides of the room and no longer associating as mother and daughter. Kanderin's love for Liadd and Arlynn's for Hurli had made them enemies of each other. Gazing at their pale tense faces, the dreamweaver wondered what kind of love it was that could be so blindly selective, so utterly divisive. She feared for them both, feared how they would react if the verdict went against them and how she would even begin to heal them.

She was soon to find out. Zuke touched her arm, whispered that Mistress Agla had finished conferring and was ready to pass judgement. Heads turned towards the door as Liadd and Hurli, their hands bound behind their backs with restraining ropes, were escorted from the ante-room to stand before the carved wooden chair in which the old woman sat.

Nemony shivered, gripped by a sudden chill. The afternoon had darkened. Thunder rumbled in the distance and a small wind whined through the open window. She rose to close it. Dull light shone on the council table as she resumed her seat, shone on the dance floor where the accused men stood. And the old woman's voice echoed among the roof vaults, pronouncing their fate.

"I have weighed the evidence submitted against you..."

"I bet you have!" snarled Liadd. "All the evidence but mine!"

"You were offered the opportunity—"

"Who would have listened? This village, along with every other, is run according to the dictates of the Dreamweavers' Guild! Every person in it is one of your lackeys, too lily-livered to speak out against you!"

"Be silent!" Zuke said sternly.

"See what I mean?" said Liadd.

The bandages were white round his ribs and his orange eyes were loaded with hate. And there was hatred in Hurli's eyes, too, but only for Liadd, hatred fostered by the dream Eth had woven, her part in the events which Mistress Agla must also take into consideration. Nemony, too, must share responsibility for the actions of the girl who had been in her charge and the old woman herself for persuading her to allow an inexperienced recruit to practise her art. For the ruination of five human lives, for all that had happened to Eth and her family, the guilt could not be Liadd's alone, nor Hurli's either. It belonged to everyone, to Kanderin for her years of acquiescence, to Arlynn for choosing the man she married, to the community in which they lived for fostering a soul capable of murder. The judgement when it came would fall on every person in the room and all, in their varying degrees, would carry the shame.

"It is with regret," Mistress Agla said quietly, "that I find the charge against both of you proven beyond doubt. You, Hurli, even allowing your claim that you acted in defence of Eth, are guilty of attempted murder against Liadd. And you, Liadd, without any mitigating circumstances, are guilty of the attempted murder of your sister. I therefore sentence you both to exile on Malroth until such a time that you be deemed fit to return."

"No!" wept Arlynn.

"No!" Kanderin said bitterly.

They rose to their feet, mother and daughter briefly united by a single emotion, willing to forgo their reasoning and their pride, to plead, beg or grovel, to do anything they could but accept the loss of the men they loved. Thunder rolled over head and rain sluiced against the windows and the Guild Mistress sat unmoved by accusations or arguments, by Kanderin's bitterness or Arlynn's tears. And deep in her soul Nemony felt the sadness begin.

They drifted through the spaces between worlds, a grey void all around them. No source of light, no external objects by which to judge distance or proximity, just speed without movement, duration without time. Eth had no way of telling how long or how far they had travelled. All she was aware of was Vashlian's hand gripping her arm and the purple brilliance of his aura eclipsing her own. The etheric shield he had raised to protect them as they left the alien spaceship remained in place, and even if she had wanted to Eth could not have escaped.

But the thought did not occur to her. She knew well enough that her physical body could not survive long without her and was grateful that Vashlian was taking her home. She had no need to ask questions, nor did she expect him to speak to her. He was simply a presence beside her, an irresistible force propelling her along. Now and then she stole a glance at him – his thin lips and hard eyes, the scar on his face and his hair hung with beads and feathers – just as she remembered. The black scarf he had worn on Malroth, as protection against the blowing sand, streamed out behind him and his black robes fluttered in the unseen winds that went rushing past them.

"How do you feel?" Vashlian finally asked her.

"Strange," she said.

"You're lucky to be alive," he informed her. "Not many survive the kind of psychic bombardment you have experienced. And what possessed you to battle with your brother? What did you hope to gain?"

Eth frowned. It was so long since she had been within her physical body sitting beneath the willan trees by the lake that she could not recall her own reasoning.

"Liadd needed help," she said uncertainly.

"And you were the one to render that help? A novice with little or no experience? Without seeking advice from either your tutor or your acolyte? Without even telling them what you were about? Whatever possessed you, girl?" His voice was not angry, merely questioning.

Yet Eth felt accused and hung her head.

"No matter," said Vashlian. "You have survived in spite of yourself. I had expected to find you adrift in the auric plane, drained and comatose…"

"I might have been if not for Troy," Eth told him.

"Which one was Troy?" he inquired.

"The boy with blue eyes."

"The one you encountered before?"

"You remember that?"

"The dream of a child that was no dream at all," murmured Vashlian. "Yes, I remember. I remembered the moment I boarded their ship. Hundreds of frozen people, not dead as you claimed them to be, but sleeping. And doubtless you noticed the state of their auras."

"Yes," said Eth.

"Damaged," said Vashlian. "Contaminated, all of them, and all of them unaware. And the boy was no different…"

"Yet he helped me," said Eth. "He gave me some of his own psychic energy and helped me survive."

"He could just as easily have destroyed you," Vashlian stated.

He could have, thought Eth, but he had not. None of them had who were awake. Despite their unstable emotions, they had all been kind to her. And Vashlian was bound to think the worst of them. Lewis had shot at him with a laser gun, acted out of fear, not knowing who he was or why he was there.

"They're not all bad," she told him.

"No more than your brother is," Vashlian retorted. "But had you spent as many years as I have on Malroth among those who are exiled there, you would know there is a point where psychic contamination becomes irreversible. I grant that many on board that ship may be redeemable, the boy among them, but even with help such as we could give them, redemption is a long slow process. And are they heading for Arbroth?"

"What if they are?" muttered Eth.

Vashlian glanced at her, and his grip on her arm tightened.

"Regard what lies ahead of us," he commanded.

She looked where he pointed and all she saw was greyness. Then two small points of colour appeared within it, a blob of brightness, a blob of dark, that grew as they approached into vast spheres haloed with contrasting light. Worlds, said Vashlian, Malroth and Arbroth viewed from the perspective of the auric plane, as Eth had never seen them before.

A stillness touched her, a small pause filled with wonder. She had never imagined a planet to be a living thing, never dreamed that each world would possess its own aura reflecting its health or sickness. But there was Arbroth, ringed with shimmering rainbows of colour, vibrant and beautiful, taking away her breath in a moment of awe as she gazed upon it – and Malroth, dull and dead, the russet glow of rocks and sand and the small greeny glitter of its marshes barely visible among the swirling, seething smog of darkness that surrounded it. The damage dealt it by the race of people from whom Eth had sprung had not healed yet, even after centuries of time.

"Do you know our history?" Vashlian asked her.

"Yes," she murmured.

"And would you risk it being repeated on Arbroth?"

"No," she admitted.

"No," agreed Vashlian. "But if the alien ship lands on our world it could easily happen. So I'll ask you again. Is Arbroth their destination?"

"They mean us no harm!" said Eth. "They gave me assurance of that."

"And you believed them?"

"Why should I not?"

"No reason," Vashlian said curtly. "And do you know how long will it take them to reach us? How long before they arrive?"

Eth regarded him suspiciously.

"Maybe they didn't tell me?" she said.

"Now answer my question!" Vashlian said harshly.

"Three years," Eth replied.

Thunder crackled out towards the lake and the cottage seemed to cower under the deluge of rain, stifling since Cable had closed the windows. He fetched water in a bowl to wet Eth's lips and sponge her face – then paused, staring at her face. Something had changed in it, although he could not have said what. A flush of life, perhaps, in the pallor of her cheeks? A sense of presence, rather than absence? To the husk of her body Eth had come home. Hardly daring to believe, Cable turned his head seeking confirmation. Vashlian, seated motionless in the rocking chair since early morning, had opened his eyes.

"You found her!" said Cable.

The man nodded, flexed his limbs and rose to approach the bed. A lean hand, with Malroth's sand encrusted beneath his fingernails, brushed away the

183

dark tendrils of hair from Eth's face.

"She should wake naturally after a while," he said. "I'm not sure how much she'll remember – or what psychic or emotional damage there will be – but hopefully she'll fully recover in time."

"Where was she?" asked Cable.

Vashlian hesitated.

"Nowhere on Arbroth or Malroth," he replied.

"Meaning I'm not to know?" asked Cable.

Rain sluiced against the window, and Vashlian made no reply.

"I *am* her acolyte," Cable said stiffly.

Vashlian nodded. "And she will tell you herself if she sees fit… or not, as the case may be. Either way, don't under-rate yourself. Few could have followed where this girl was, certainly no acolyte I am acquainted with. Stay with her, boy, whatever happens. She'll have need of you before the next three years are out. And bring her to the Academy as soon as she recovers."

Cable stared at him as he wrapped the protective scarf round his face and head. "Suppose she doesn't want to go?"

"Then persuade her," Vashlian told him.

"How?" asked Cable.

"How is not my concern," Vashlian retorted. "But if you care about the future of this planet, boy, you'll

184

do as I ask."

Then he was gone, heading back towards the trans-matt terminal, a dark shape striding through the rain. Thunder growled and fork-lightning flickered and unanswered questions whirled in Cable's head. Behind him Eth sighed in her sleep and he wanted to shake her, wake her, command her to tell him what he wanted to know – but the front door opened and Nemony came rushing in. Rain trickled from her hair, dripped from her soaked clothes and pooled on the floor at her feet, and her orange eyes shone with a mixture of joy and relief.

"I've just met Vashlian," she said breathlessly. "He said he found her, said she has returned to her body. He thinks she's going to recover, thinks she'll be all right." She approached the bed, gazed down at Eth's sleeping face. "Is it true?" she whispered. "Is she really with us again? And when she wakes what do we tell her?"

Her expression clouded, the joy in her eyes changing to sorrow when she turned to look at Cable. "They are gone," she told him. "Her whole family have gone. Kanderin and Arlynn... her mother and sister... they chose to go with Liadd and Hurli, chose to be exiled on Malroth and I could not dissuade them. There is no one left on Arbroth for Eth."

"Except us," said Cable.

Nemony shook her head.

"Not even us," she said brokenly. "Surely you realise? Eth can never be a dreamweaver, not after this. We could have forgiven the dream she wove for Hurli, put it down to her immaturity, a sudden lapse in her self-control. But with Liadd she broke the rules, knowingly and deliberately. Lives have been ruined because of it, including her own. The Academy won't have her, Cable. Not even Mistress Agla will speak up for her now."

"But Vashlian will," Cable said quietly.

Nemony looked at him dubiously. "What say does Vashlian have?" she inquired.

"I don't know," said Cable. "But he told me to take her to the Academy as soon as she's well." And in the dreamweaver's eyes he saw a little surge of hope.

CHAPTER SIXTEEN

Days and nights for Eth became a muddle of sleep and dreams and brief awakenings where Cable, or Nemony, fed or washed or turned her and all the memories she had of that time were erased by exhaustion and the need to sleep again. Then, gradually, the periods of wakefulness lengthened. She became more aware of where she was and who was with her, of her physical body grown weak and thin and covered with bed sores. She remembered Nemony bathing her, the feel of warm water and the fragrance of rillroses, the sharp astringent scent of ointment. She remembered the taste of fish stew and shote's milk, herb tea and tonic wine tangy with iron. She learned to walk again with Cable's help, just a few shaky steps from the bed to the rocking chair, and sat for long hours staring through the window at the shorn meadows and the mountains rising beyond.

Summer was gone. Clouds and sunlight made shadows on the land, burlberries fruited and fire daisies bloomed in scarlet masses on the open slopes. Dusk came early with a hint of frost. The Roth Star set behind the Edderhorn in a blaze of sunset light and Malroth, in the mornings, was a dull red orb seen through the mists that drifted inland from the lake. The days grew chill and Cable kept the fire burning in the bedroom.

Then, as Eth grew stronger, she was able to move around the house unaided and help with a few household chores. She took her meals in the kitchen and spent the long evenings sitting in the inglenook, knitting socks by firelight as the roof slates cracked with cold or the wind whined outside in the first slight snowfall of the season. It was a quiet companionable time. Brenner made music on a reed flute. Nemony sat spinning and Cable whittled wooden animals for the village children from scraps of wood.

And sometimes they talked... about this and that; about Nemony learning to dreamweave and how necessary was her time at the Academy; and what it was like there according to Cable's reminiscences. They talked of what went on in the village, too. Life, Eth learned, was pretty much the same although she had no part in it. Morning and evening the shoteherders drove their flocks along the stony path to and from the mountain pastures and the school bell rang daily, summoning the children to their lessons. Men, in the evenings, gathered at the tavern as they always did and at night Nemony continued to ply her trade. She learned that Zella was expecting another child, that the widow Olna seemed set to wed the tavern-keeper's brother the following spring, that peddlers were now coming regularly through the trans-matt terminal trading in unusual trinkets. But all of that had nothing to do with Eth and there was never any mention of her own family, of Arlynn and Kanderin, Liadd and Hurli, and how they fared.

She began to suspect that Cable and Nemony were keeping things from her, just as she was keeping things from them. She could understand her own reluctance to share what she had experienced. Her bond with Troy confused her still, and the fact that there was an alien spaceship on its way to Arbroth had best not be made common knowledge, Vashlian had warned her. Eth had reasons for her reticence, but she could not understand what reasons Cable and Nemony had. She grew more and more aware of it –

odd breaks in their conversation and deliberate changes of subject, strange silences and surreptitious glances, a conspiracy of silence. She grew to fear what they were hiding but, finally, she was bound to ask.

"What happened when I was away, Nemony?"

It was late afternoon. Sleety rain veiled the mountains and the dreamweaver had recently emerged from her room after a day of sleep. Brenner was chopping kindling in the shed and Eth and Cable were crumbling bunches of dried herbs into clay storage pots. The kitchen was full of scents of lovegloss and dreamwort, fire logs burning and stew in the cauldron cooking for supper. Nemony speared a slice of bread with a long fork and held it to toast by the fire.

"How do you mean?" she inquired.

"I mean, what happened here in the village?" said Eth.

"Nothing," Cable said hurriedly.

"Then why aren't you telling me?" asked Eth.

"Because there's nothing to tell," Cable said logically.

"But there must be something," Eth argued. "What happened to Liadd? Why hasn't my mother been to visit me? Or Arlynn?"

"They're away," said Cable.

"Away where? What do you mean?"

Nemony sighed. "She has to know sometime, Cable."

They had kept it from her out of kindness, until she was well enough to know and strong enough to bear it. They were gone, all of them, Liadd and Hurli exiled to Malroth, Arlynn and Kanderin choosing to accompany them. And Eth, too, when she was fully recovered would have to leave the village.

Nemony had done her best to break it to her gently. She had cradled her in her arms and let her cry, soothed and comforted and explained. What had happened was not Eth's fault, she said. She was not to blame for what Liadd had done to her, for Arlynn's misplaced loyalty or Kanderin's self-imposed banishment, for the hatred that had driven Hurli to wield the knife. They were all responsible for their own actions. And the termination of her apprenticeship, her dismissal from the dreamweaver's employ, was not a punishment. Nemony loved her dearly, but she had taught her all she could. It was time for her to move on and there was a place waiting for her at the Academy.

"It's not the end of the world," said Nemony.

"More like a new beginning," Cable said earnestly.

But Eth was inconsolable.

It was the end of the world for Liadd and Hurli,

Arlynn and Kanderin, the end of their lives on Arbroth. And that was her fault, no matter what Nemony said. If it had not been for her malpractice and interference they would still be living in the house in the village, not struggling to survive on a desert planet among the ruins of a past civilisation.

She went to her room, cried for hours, but no amount of tears could wash away her guilt and no words of Cable's could make her see things differently. He gave up in the end, slept on his pallet in the shuttered alcove, and she lay awake condemning herself. She had caused the ruination of four other lives, caused her own kindred to be sent into exile – and even if they returned after serving their sentences, they would not forgive her, no more than she would forgive herself.

Over and over the thoughts churned in her head, branching off into diverse directions as the firelight flickered on the bedroom walls and Cable snored. Who controls the dream, controls the man, he had told her. But Eth no longer wanted to control anyone's dreams. The responsibility was more than she could bear, the consequences of failure too appalling. Nemony was right to terminate her apprenticeship. And what was the point in going to Academy to study for a career of which she was afraid?

Yet, if she did not go to the Academy, there would be nothing left for her. Cable would be assigned to someone else and Eth would be alone and purposeless, belonging nowhere, an alien in her own world, as alien as Troy would be when the spaceship landed. But maybe it never would, she thought wretchedly. Maybe, in the three years that remained, Vashlian would find a way to prevent it. And Eth would never know, for to those outside its order the Dreamweavers' Guild seldom divulged its secrets.

Unless she returned to the ship? she thought. She could not stay there, of course, not for three years without her body. But she could visit at regular intervals and monitor its progress. Help counteract, perhaps, whatever Vashlian planned? Her abilities remained and no one could stop her using them. She could dream-walk whenever she wanted to, even though she was no longer a dreamweaver. She could go to Malroth, too, find her mother and seek out Arlynn and Hurli, make her peace and do what she could for them, some small reparation for her crime.

Grey dawn showed between the cracks in the curtains and sleet lashed the window as Eth rose from her bed. Quietly, so as not to disturb Cable, she added logs to the fire and seated herself in the rocking chair. It had been many weeks since she last travelled with Vashlian through the auric plane, longer since she had left her body of her own free will, on a summer night sitting beneath the willans beside the lake.

Nerves in her stomach tightened as she remembered and when she closed her eyes the scene with Liadd replayed itself within her head. Fear drained her of courage, made it impossible for her to relax. She had to concentrate on her breathing, consciously control it, count the slow inhalations and exhalations... wait for her mind to grow still and empty... wait for the sweet, familiar, floating, drifting feeling of her dream-body about to make the shift. Then someone clapped a hand on her shoulder.

"Oh no you don't!" said Cable.

With a small shriek Eth was shocked into wakefulness, but Cable showed no remorse. He stood before her, his hands on his hips, firelight glinting on his nose-stud, anger in his eyes. And she cringed at the lash of his voice.

"Are you stupid or out of your mind?" Cable asked wrathfully. "You're not recovered enough yet to take off on another psychic adventure! Just a single trip will be enough to sap whatever energy you've regained! And you ought to have more sense than to sneak away on your own for a second time without telling me! Just what does it take for you to learn?"

"I wasn't thinking," Eth muttered.

"You weren't thinking last time either!" snapped Cable. "And where were you off to anyway?"

"Nowhere," said Eth.

"Meaning you've no intention of telling me? No more than you've told me where you went before? A dreamweaver is supposed to trust her acolyte, Eth!"

"I'm not a dreamweaver!" said Eth. "I've been dismissed, remember? And what I do now is nothing to do with you!"

"Isn't it?" said Cable. "I still care, you know! And what about the Academy?"

"I'm not going," Eth said bitterly.

"What do you mean, you're not going?"

Cable stared at her.

And all over again his rage exploded.

"You can't make a decision like that, Eth, without even discussing it! What about me? Hasn't it occurred to you that I'll be affected by what you do? If you quit, I'm going to be re-assigned! I could end up serving some malicious power-drunk old crone in a stinking marsh miles from anywhere! Or dragging a sledge across the tundra for a travelling shaman! Well, thanks very much, and so much for friendship! Next time you get stranded in the auric plane you can damn well stay there!"

He sounded like Troy, except that his complaints were justified.

And yet again Eth was at fault.

She hung her head, chewed her lip, and tried to reason. But she was torn in too many directions, torn between Arbroth and Malroth and a ship full of aliens, between Troy and Cable and her own exiled family. Whatever she did, and however much she loved, she caused too much hurt and too many losses. She was afraid of herself. Afraid, if she went to the Academy, of what might be asked of her and the damage she might do. Slow tears trickled down her cheeks. Her life lay in ruins around her and there was nothing she could do to set things right.

"Go away!" she whimpered.

But instead of going, Cable put his arms round her, rocked her like a child and stroked her hair.

"Listen, Eth. Listen to what I say. These last four years have been good years, right? You've grown a lot and learned a lot, and what you are has come to matter, both to me and Nemony. We can't let you throw it all away for nothing. You're going to the Academy, whether you want to or not. And whatever's happened you're going to have to face it – and face yourself. You don't have to do it alone. I'll help you. But first you have to tell me where you were when I couldn't find you and what happened there. Eth? Are you listening?"

"Vashlian told me not to say anything," she

murmured.

"But he didn't mean to me," said Cable.

She sighed deeply and began to speak. And Cable listened, questioned, prompted her gently when she faltered. She told him everything, except what had happened between herself and Troy. That was private, she decided. Her bond with him was nothing to do with Cable. But it remained the emotive force behind her story, the root of her fear, and maybe he suspected. It was not just a ship full of aliens that concerned her. Not just the fact she had been there and Vashlian had found her and would probably try to prevent their landing, that was the cause of her anguish. It was grief for yet another loss, as deep and as searing and the loss of her mother and sister and brother, something she could never tell to anyone.

"So you met him again?" Cable said quietly.

"Who?" said Eth.

"The boy with blue eyes."

"What boy with blue eyes?"

Cable glanced up at her.

"The one you met as a child, Eth. The one you told me about the first night I arrived here."

"I'd forgotten about him," Eth lied.

Cable's eyes turned hard and there was a harsh edge to his voice. "In that case I don't understand you," he said curtly. "And nothing you've told me makes any sense. Vashlian's not likely to destroy those people, is he? The worst he can do is coerce whoever's on board and divert the ship elsewhere, and what's that to you? You surely don't *want* it to land? Three thousand emotionally unstable, psychically damaged aliens? What effect will that have on our culture, Eth? It'll be *we* who are destroyed!"

Wearily, Eth stared at the feeble remains of the fire. She had been awake all night and was too tired to argue. Cable did not understand, probably never would, and that was that. But he had not finished with her yet.

"It's time you got your head together," he told her. "You've got to forget it, put behind you everything that's happened. The fate of that ship and whatever Vashlian does is not your responsibility. You've got your own life to live, your own future to think of. And if you can't forget, then go to the Academy, learn to use and apply whatever powers you possess and do something about it yourself! If those alien people matter so much to you then why not learn to heal them as you failed to heal Liadd, perhaps? Maybe, in the three years they are heading towards us, you can fit them to join us on Arbroth... and someone at the Academy can surely teach you."

He rose from the hearth rug on which he had been

sitting, limped to the window and drew back the curtains. The long night was over. Morning light flooded the room, sunlight on snow, a chill cutting through her, fierce and invigorating as his words. In a quick bright moment of hope Eth looked towards him.

"Could I really do that?" she asked.

He turned to regard her.

"You can do anything you want to, except give up," he said.

CHAPTER SEVENTEEN

A new beginning, Cable had said. And a chance to help Troy, thought Eth. But first came the wrench of parting with Nemony, the pain and the loss. Tears on her cheeks mingled with the rain as she walked to the village, following Cable and Brenner, who was carrying the bags. A new beginning. People came from the houses to bid her goodbye and she carried their warm wishes and well-loved faces with her... Zuke and Zella and Yordan... and the place and the landscape, mountains lost among cloud, and the house where she had been born. It was abandoned and empty, containing, as she did, nothing but memories now. There was nothing left for her in the village, Cable had said. Just the great black pyramid in the centre of the square, the trans-matt terminal opening to receive her, a rectangle of light making watery reflections on the cobbles. Brenner set down her travel bag on the threshold and turned towards her.

"G...good luck, M...Miss Eth," he stammered.

He was the last person Eth saw as Cable ushered her inside... a man she had grown to love and respect standing outside in the winter rain, his eyes wet as hers, before the door to the trans-matt slid shut. And this was not the beginning. This was the end. She turned to face it. Grid-maps on the walls showing the trans-matt system on Arbroth, names of places with their corresponding transit numbers, a panel with the operating buttons beside the door. The old black sarcophagus Eth had once feared stood small and black in the centre of the floor, a pyramid within a pyramid. She dashed a hand across her eyes. From here she could go anywhere, complete with her physical body, except where she wanted to go – back to the space ship.

"We could go to Malroth," she suggested.

"If you know the transit number," said Cable.

"Isn't it listed?"

"Most people never need to know it," said Cable. "Now, do you have any more bright suggestions or shall we go to the Academy?"

Eth shrugged, and Cable entered the transit code. A red light above the door flashed a warning. The walls blurred and vanished – or maybe Eth herself vanished, became swallowed up in a vortex of whiteness, moments of nothing and nowhere, the end of everything. And after the end came the new beginning, the inescapable destination. Everything reformed around her. The door opened, Cable picked up the bags, and Eth stepped out of a different trans-matt terminal, a different person in a different place.

For Eth it truly was a new beginning but she did not find it easy to adapt. Among a myriad buildings and a thousand other students, bound to a routine that she did not know, all she was aware of was her own bewilderment. Days became a confusion of dim rooms and outside heat, strange voices, strange faces, lessons she could not understand and the heady scents of flowers. Night fell suddenly, brief flaring sunsets that gave way to velvet darkness and tropical stars. And Malroth hung low and huge above the northern horizon and was gone before dawn. Anthems of frogs and crickets, and heavy rain drumming on the roof of the housing block, kept her from sleeping. She suffered from heat rash and tropical fruits gave her the squits.

It would take a while for her to acclimatise, Cable informed her. And she would have been lost without him, miserable and alone. Younger by years than the other trainees, and not part of the annual intake, she was assigned to a class of first-year students that was already established. Friendships between groups of novice dreamweavers and their acolytes had been formed without her and, socially, she was uninvolved. And the tutors made her nervous, black-gowned women and grey-gowned men who questioned even her right to be there.

Many claimed she was far too young to understand the subjects they taught – behavioural psychology, communal morality, intra-dimensional communication, social ecology and human ethics. Yet, in more practical subjects, she was far in advance. She knew her herb lore, the properties and dosages of recognised plants. She was able to view human auras, diagnose disease and debility and emotional states from the variations of colour. And she had learned to dream-walk where most of the others had not, was able to slip from her body and range throughout the auric plane across distances few could follow. She could even translate into the physical dimension, her dream image appearing before the class as a demonstration.

To some of the tutors her abilities were made

more impressive by her lack of maturity. And there were others, too – shadowy Masters and Mistresses of the Dreamweavers' Guild who lurked in the background and insisted she remain at the Academy. Those who objected to her presence were over-ruled, although the reason why was never stated and Eth herself was unaware.

Weeks passed and she saw neither Vashlian nor Mistress Agla. Memories of her old life had begun to fade and they along with it, although now and then she sent a message to Nemony through the trans-matt system, or gazed at the night stars and thought of Troy, remembering her purpose for being there. And now and then she stared at the orange orb of Malroth rising beyond the lake, re-experiencing her guilt and wondered how they were, Kanderin and Liadd, Arlynn and Hurli.

But mostly her mind was occupied in study, poring over books borrowed from the Academy library in an attempt to come to grips with the subjects she found difficult, the lessons of the day she had failed to comprehend. And again, if it had not been for Cable, she would have been lost.

Potential acolytes were usually granted admission to the Academy at a much younger age than potential dreamweavers. Many, lacking certain aptitudes, were culled and rejected by the tutors themselves and never began the more advanced stages of their training. Others, for various reasons, were rejected by the young women they were assigned to and many more were capable of offering their dreamweaver only a limited service. But Eth was lucky – she had Cable.

As with all trainee dreamweavers and their acolytes, they were given adjoining rooms in one of the housing blocks, expected to spend time together and form a solid working relationship. And much of what Eth struggled to grasp was revision to Cable. He was able to understand what she could not and, in the evenings, he would sit beside her on the balcony as the rain sluiced down and the day's heat turned to coolness, patiently explaining and elucidating.

More and more Eth grew to depend on him. Cable, her only friend, always there, always at her side. In the mêlée of the dining hall he fetched her fruit and salad. He came to comfort her when bad dreams woke her in the night and on free days kept her company, limping beside her along the margins of the lake. He was extrovert in the face of her shyness, helping her to overcome it. And of an age with her fellow students, he was more accepted, making friends easily and taking her to small social gatherings, starlit swimming parties, evening debates and role-playing dramas, gradually integrating her into the life of the Academy.

Finally, Eth began to enjoy herself and regained her confidence. The occasional frowns of the tutors ceased to bother her. The lectures she had once found so meaningless and boring began to interest her. No dreamweaver could be responsible for the foibles and failings of another person, she was taught. Life's lessons were theirs for the learning but if, through the dreams she wove, she could offer a solution to their problems or add to their understanding of themselves and others, then her work would not be in vain.

And there was one basic rule to remember, the tutor announced, when deciding whether or not to commence treating someone without their knowledge, permission and co-operation. All individuals were free to do as they wished. But if what they did harmed the planet they lived on, the ecological balance of its flora and fauna, or any other sentient form of life then they forfeited that freedom and psychic restraints became necessary.

Suddenly Eth realised the value of ethics. Both Liadd and Hurli had broken that rule and she was absolved of her guilt in a single moment of comprehension. And when darkness fell, she walked through the gardens with a group of comrades, laughing and talking beneath a sky crowded with more distant stars.

Unseen among them, the ship carrying Troy was one day nearer. And would its passengers really harm Arbroth if they landed? she wondered. This warm wonderful world that seemed in that moment as perfect as her life?

Seasons passed, indistinguishable from each other in that tropical clime. One year became another and Eth began to grow impatient. Apart from academics, she had as yet learned nothing to advance her healing skills, nor how to combat the kind of psychic assault Liadd had inflicted on her. Without that knowledge she had no hope of helping Troy or any of the people on board the space ship. And the link between her and Troy, that had twice before drawn her towards him, seemed to have vanished. However far across the auric plain Eth travelled, she never found her way back to the ship.

By then, all the girls in Eth's class could dream-walk but none as well as Eth herself. At some far point she always left them behind. But usually they stayed together within the planetary field, gradually travelling further and further from the Academy grounds. It was Eth herself who taught them to translate into the physical dimension. Then, by practising what they had learned in the intra-dimensional communication classes, they were able to transmit what they saw back to their acolytes – telepathic images of frozen lakes and snow-covered tundra beyond the northern mountains; stilt villages built around the southern swamps; unnamed creatures bathing in remote mud wallows or lumbering through impenetrable jungles; images of waterfalls and cataracts, forest and farmland, lakeside towns and hidden valleys.

And once at dawn, alone and wakeful when Cable was sleeping, Eth visited the village at the foot of the Edderhorn and the house where she had been born. It was derelict and decaying, its roof shingles slipped to let in the rain, its shutters fallen, doors and windows rotting away and the once neat garden choked with weeds. No one wanted it – a house haunted by blood and violence, by the unhappiness of those who had lived in it. It was left to die as the surrounding woods unfurled their leaves and the alpine meadows bloomed with fresh spring flowers. It revived Eth's memories, restored a pain in her she thought she had forgotten. And things happening at the Academy troubled her, too. She had begun to dreamweave again, just simple elementary dreams of which Cable was the recipient, yet each nightly session became a fear she had to force herself to face.

Unlike the majority of the other trainees, Eth had no etheric guide, no spirit from the higher dimensions to feed her the images she needed or whisper words of advice in her mind. Along with Nemony, she was one of a minority of dreamweavers who had only herself to rely on, and she feared the responsibility, the past experience of her own failure. For her, the tutor said, a thorough grounding in ethics and psychology was vitally important and consultation with her acolyte was not only advisable but necessary, because she alone would be answerable for every decision she ever made.

"And that's what scares me," Eth confessed later to a group of students that had gathered for an evening debate. "I just don't trust myself to that extent."

"And you obviously don't trust me either," said Cable.

Eth leaned on the rail of the veranda.

"That's not what I said!"

"But you don't find consultation easy," Cable reminded her. "You never have. You don't talk things out. You just make up your mind and carry on doing things without telling me, going places without telling me – like the other morning, for example. Where did you go then when I was asleep?"

"Nowhere," muttered Eth.

"I woke as you returned," said Cable.

"Surely you must have been mistaken?" one young woman murmured. "No dreamweaver would go travelling without confiding in her acolyte, Cable. And you and Eth have always seemed so close."

"Eth's close all right," Cable informed her.

Eth's hands tightened on the rail of the balcony. Malroth, baleful and bright, hung low above the jungle on the opposite shore. All over again she was forced to remember – four people lived in exile there because of her, and because of her a ship among the stars, coming ever closer, might never arrive. She had betrayed its presence, betrayed Troy, and she feared what would become of him, just as she feared for her family. And how could she share that fear with Cable? How could she make him responsible for what she had done? Voices talked about her behind her back.

"What we fear in ourselves, we also fear in other people," someone said. "So, if Eth's afraid of taking responsibility then she's not going to share it with anyone else, is she? Nor will she accept anyone else's decisions – neither yours, Cable, nor the decisions of the Dreamweavers' Guild, nor an etheric guide's, either."

Cable chuckled. "Which probably explains why she hasn't got one! You can't hide things from an etheric guide. They see right through you and Eth couldn't cope with that kind of openness."

Eth swung to face him, his tawny eyes and gold nose stud shining in the lantern light. She knew she was responsible for her own feelings, but he was making her feel wrong, turning against her as once she had turned against herself. Emotions she would rather not own churned inside her.

"What do you know about it?" she raged at him. "What do you know about being responsible! You're just an acolyte, Cable! I'm the one who has to make the decisions and live with the results! I don't want to be a dreamweaver and I didn't want to come to the Academy either! That was your idea! You pushed me into it! And for what?"

She allowed him no chance to reply, nor for anyone else to intercede. She just turned on her heel and left the balcony, hurried along the gravel path towards the trans-matt terminal. She did not know where she would go but she wanted to escape from the Academy and everyone who knew her, from the fear that was within her and the future she could not foresee. Black under the starlight the pyramid loomed before her in the gravel courtyard. But the doorway opened as she reached it and someone emerged, stood before her on the threshold, a man in black robes in a rectangle of light. Hard eyes fixed on Eth's face.

"We meet yet again," Vashlian said softly.

CHAPTER EIGHTEEN

It was a chance encounter that prevented Eth from leaving. Waylaid by Vashlian in the doorway to the trans-matt terminal, she was unable to enter without pushing past him and revealing her intent. And maybe he knew anyway, his psychic eyes fixed on hers, reading the emotions of her aura, reading her mind.

"I see you are recovered from your previous ordeal," Vashlian remarked. "And who, now, are you attempting to escape from? The Academy or yourself?"

Eth tried to still the nervous hammering of her heart. She knew from experience Vashlian would know if she lied. "The Academy," she informed him.

"And why is that?" he inquired.

"Because it has nothing more to teach me that I want to know," Eth replied.

Vashlian unwound the black scarf from round his head and raised an eyebrow. "Is that so?" he questioned. "Yet your aura has changed – violet flares surround the green – and your powers have increased. It must have taught you something. And if you leave, where will you go and what will you do?"

Eth shrugged.

"I don't know," she muttered.

"You don't know?" mocked Vashlian. "And shall I tell you? It's a powerful bond that draws a dreamweaver to her place. But what draws you, girl? Nothing on Arbroth, is it? Your links here are severed. And what does that leave you? Just the alien boy and his people travelling between stars aboard a ship you cannot find, and your family on Malroth – problematical, all of them, and needing help. And if you would learn to deal with psychic contamination, and learn to defend yourself against it, you could do worse than work on Malroth with me."

Eth stared at him, and the prospect appalled her. "Go into exile?" she questioned. "Live among people who maim and murder?"

Vashlian smiled, but not with his eyes.

"Men like your father and brother," he said.

"People like the boy on the spaceship, aliens to our culture on Arbroth. Would you have them damned for ever for their aberrant natures, their mistaken thinking? Or would you prefer to help them? I told you before: few are beyond redemption, although redemption takes time. And how can Malroth be exile for those who choose freely to go there? Think on it, girl. We need dreamweavers on Malroth and it is a possible future for you."

Eth wanted to scream at him that she did not want to be a dreamweaver, but instead her voice fell to a whisper. "Who *are* you?" she asked.

"What I have always been," Vashlian replied. "And you would be similar, I suspect, if only you stop being afraid of yourself."

"I don't know what you mean," said Eth.

But Vashlian was no longer looking at her, he was looking beyond her to where Cable came limping towards them, a look that was strange and significant, that Eth did not understand. Then with a nod at the youth who was her acolyte, Vashlian strode away towards the Administration block.

"What did *he* want?" asked Cable.

"Who *is* he?" Eth repeated.

"Officially," said Cable, "the Guild employs him in an advisory capacity. Or else he employs the Guild. And the Institute of Sciences as well, probably. Rumours label him as some kind of visionary. So what were you two talking about?"

"Nothing much," Eth said crossly.

"Meaning you're not prepared to tell me yet again?" asked Cable.

"It was nothing to do with you," said Eth.

"As usual," Cable said coldly.

But he was later to find out at least some of it.

Vashlian must have reported Eth's discontentment with the Academy, for the next morning she and Cable were sent for. They were interviewed separately. Cable was the first to be called from the psychology lecture and Eth, on his return, was summoned to the Administration block.

From there a black-gowned Mistress escorted her to a quiet sunlit quadrangle bright with flowers, where closed glass doors led into dim apartments. Outside one that was open, the Mistress stopped.

"Do go in," she said.

"Yes, do come in, my dear," confirmed an ancient voice.

It was not the official interview that Eth had expected. Sitting beside Mistress Agla in a wicker chair, gazing out at the quadrangle gardens, sipping iced tea and talking, was pleasant and relaxing. Eth saw rich woven rugs on the floor, paintings hanging on the walls, a multi-coloured counterpane on the bed, a carved chest, decorated vases, a chiming clock, knick-knacks and ornaments too numerous to define. Gifts gathered over the years, Mistress Agla said. And this was the place she always returned to, hers for her lifetime, the only home she had.

"It's what everyone needs," the old woman murmured. "Somewhere secure, somewhere to be alone in without being lonely, to be ourselves as well as being a part of something bigger. Here is where I belong, I suppose."

"It's lovely," Eth said wistfully.

"And where do you belong, Eth?"

"Have you been talking to Vashlian?" asked Eth.

Mistress Agla nodded. "He told me you are less than happy here," she said. "And Cable tells me you fear the responsibilities involved in being a dreamweaver. You don't, however, have to become a dreamweaver to stay at the Academy and remain with the Dreamweavers' Guild. You have considerable talents, Eth, and there are other ways you can put them to use. You could eventually become one of our many advisors, perhaps? Dreamweavers and acolytes, throughout Arbroth, often need an independent counsellor. Or you could become a travelling adjudicator, as I have done. Or join our administrative staff, perhaps? Or become a tutor, maybe? Your fellow students speak highly of all they have learned from you."

"Or go to Malroth?" said Eth.

"That too," the old woman agreed. "You have strong connections there to fuel your sense of purpose – much to give wherever you go, Eth. But before you make any decision to leave us, I have a proposition to put to you that is well worth considering."

Eth stared at her. Her voice was soft and cajoling and her fierce orange eyes were misted and gentle, an old coercer using her influence, about to bend Eth to her will. And whatever the proposition was, she already knew she would have no option but to agree.

After that day her position altered. She was no longer a full-time student in her last year at the Academy, but a part-time member of the staff, although she refused the offer of a staff apartment similar to Mistress Agla's. She remained in the housing block where she had always been and still attended many of the lectures, psychology, social ecology and ethics in particular. But, under the auspices of Master-Tutor Gerridon, she taught several groups of trainee dreamweavers as well, over a hundred pupils in all.

They were all older than she was, selected for their abilities from various classes throughout the Academy and assigned to her as part of an experimental programme. For his part, Master Gerridon would instruct the acolytes and Eth would coach the dreamweavers. She was to teach them what she had taught the students in her own class – all the various out-of-body skills which she herself possessed – how to travel through the auric plain beyond the immediate vicinity, how to translate their dream-bodies into the physical dimension and how to transmit back to their acolytes, across an ever increasing distance, the telepathic images of what they saw.

"These young women are the cream of the Academy," Master Gerridon said enthusiastically. "But none are as gifted as you, my dear, and none but you can teach them. We want dreamweavers who know no bounds, who can dream-walk where they will to whatever destination, who can communicate with their acolytes from whatever distance and in whatever circumstances. Can you do that, Eth?"

"I can try," Eth replied.

"You can also succeed," declared Master Gerridon.

For Eth it was a kind of freedom. Far and wide, throughout the coming seasons, she roamed across the distant reaches of Arbroth, and the bevy of dreamweavers followed her, gradually increasing their abilities. And, in training them, Eth also trained herself and Cable. She, as well as they, learned how to control the speed and direction of her journeying and how to distinguish between her own thoughts and her acolyte's telepathic voice in her mind. She learned to receive directions from Cable and reliably reach a destination she herself had not chosen. And Cable meanwhile, in response to Master Gerridon's tuition on the ground, grew aware of her smallest deviation from any pre-set pathway and learned to track her wherever she went. Never again would she be able to lose herself, he declared, and nor could she ever escape him.

"Why should I want to?" she asked.

"With you I'm never sure," Cable replied.

One of the dreamweavers laughed.

"It's great when we're all together!" she said. "I'm beginning to feel that we can go anywhere and do anything."

"What do you do in the classes when I'm not with you?" Eth asked curiously.

"Aspects of dreamweaving, mostly," the young woman informed her. "Image creation... emotive transmission... dreamweaving in unison. That kind of thing. And we're practising telekinesis as well, the influence of mind over matter – shifting the hands of a clock and snuffing out a light. If we work together we can levitate solid objects several times our own weight. But mostly it's dreamweaving. You should join us, Eth."

"That'll be the day!" retorted Cable.

Of dreamweaving Eth did not want to know. Nor did it occur to her to question Master Gerridon on the reason behind the new experimental disciplines or ask what purpose they might serve. However kindly he seemed, he was far older than she was, old enough to be her father in fact. And, like her father, he was big and burly and bearded, and she was a little in awe of him. Or perhaps a little afraid? She just did as he bade her, leading the groups of dreamweavers further and further afield. They left the surface of Arbroth all together, viewed it from auric space – a living world surrounded by a nimbus of rainbow light, its beauty aweing them into silence and aweing their acolytes, too, when they received the transmitted image. Again and again they dream-walked outwards, a daily exercise that took them in different directions towards the stars.

"Left, ten degrees." Cable's silent instructions came clearly into Eth's mind, not words exactly, but a thought or an impulse that did not spring from any source within herself. She turned in response, almost instinctively, as did the dreamweavers who were with her, each of them obeying the instructions of their own acolytes. And again, almost instinctively, she and they transmitted what they saw – nothing but grey empty space and pin-prick stars in a multitude of rainbow colours.

"Left, five degrees and advance," said Cable. It was an odd experiment, thought Eth, each separate group, day after day, fanning through sections of the immediate galaxy as if they were searching for something. And even as she thought it, their excited voices broke the silence of the auric plain.

"What's that up ahead?"

"What is it?"

"Do you see it, Eth?"

Thirty-five dusky arms pointed to a vague shadowy shape in distance. Thirty-five minds transmitted what they saw. A meteor, perhaps, composed of stone or metal, rusty red in colour and approaching rapidly, growing as it did so, becoming more and more huge, looming directly in their pathway and assuming definition. Not a meteor after all but something else, something smooth and metallic, insectoid in shape, lights shining from within it – minuscule blue ones along the side of it and domed yellow in front.

"Translate," said the thoughts in Eth's head that came from Cable. "Translate into the physical dimension. We need to see it more clearly. We need to see what it is."

She did, and so did the others, and then she

recognised what she saw – the alien spaceship framed by the distant constellations, towering metal walls bearing down on her and the dreamweavers floating around it, small as gnats in the almighty shadow of its bulk. Thoughts and voices besieged her.

"You're not transmitting!" said Cable.

"What is it?" shrilled the dreamweavers.

"What is that thing?"

"Eth!" said Cable. "You're not transmitting! I can't see—"

"It's a ship!" cried the dreamweavers.

"A ship from another world!"

"Move back from it a little."

"Our acolytes need to see the surrounding stars."

"Eth?" said Cable. "I know you can hear me and Master Gerridon has told me what you're seeing. He says you're to translate on board it."

"Translate on board it!" the dreamweavers echoed. And their excitement grew.

"Come on! Let's go!" they urged.

"No!" wailed Eth.

"Why not?" they asked.

"Because I've already been there! I already know what I'll see!"

But the rest of the dreamweavers did not and, obeying the instructions from their acolytes, one by one they faded from sight. Desperately, Eth followed, her insubstantial form slipping through the spaceship's metal bulwark before shifting back into the physical dimension again.

She found herself on the bridge with a couple of others, standing ghostly under the harsh lights among the banks of computers. Pale people stared at her – thirty or forty, she could not count how many – and the alarm sirens wailed. She looked for Troy, but she did not see him. Just Verity, in her scarlet uniform, elbowing her way through the crowd and calling her name. But Eth had no time to speak to her, no time to explain what she was doing there. Laser weapons fired from the gantry and the screams of dreamweavers elsewhere in the ship reached her across the ether. The ones around her panicked and faded and Cable howled in her head.

"Get out of there, Eth!"

Verity's voice rose to a shriek.

"You men hold your fire! They're girls, for Christ's sake! They're not here to harm us! And someone tell Wynn-Stanley to resuscitate Troy! I want him here, now, at the double!" She turned to Eth. "What are you doing here, Eth? What's going on? Who are... who were your friends?"

Eth might have remained, but she was linked to her flesh-and-blood body by a silver thread and Cable had a hold on it. Slowly, inexorably, his mental and psychic powers were dragging her away and, unable to counteract his intention, she was obliged to go with him, forced to translate into the auric plain again and leave the ship behind.

Verity was gone. Her chance of meeting Troy again was gone. The ship receded into shadow and was swallowed up by the grey auric distances as Cable hauled her back towards her body. She felt sad and weepy, as if she was being denied something she dearly wanted. The auric stars were unseeable and Arbroth's shimmering aura was blurred by her tears. And the tears remained in her eyes when she finally returned, a flesh-and-blood person sitting in a meditation chair among a class full of others. A cacophony of voices surrounded her, the shrill voices of the dreamweavers retelling their experiences and the voices of acolytes speculating and exclaiming.

"Did you see them?"

"Did you see those people?"

"They were not like us."

"Did you see the different colours of their eyes?"

"And the different colours of their faces?"

"And did you see the sleeping ones?"

"Thousands there were."

"Thousands of frozen people."

"And their auras were all dark – all damaged."

"Why did they attack us with those strange

weapons?"

"Were they trying to destroy us?"

"Who were they anyway?"

"And what are they doing there?"

"Does anyone know?"

"Later! Later!" shouted Master Gerridon. "When we've had time to assimilate your experiences we shall all know!" Smiling broadly and rubbing his hands, he crossed the room to where Eth was sitting. "Excellent! Excellent, my dear! The first part of our experiment has succeeded. We have found what we were looking for – found the alien ship. Vashlian will be pleased indeed when I tell him."

Suddenly, gazing up at him, Eth understood. It was a plot, all of it, instigated by Vashlian for the sole purpose of locating the spaceship. And unknowingly, unwittingly, Eth had found it. And now they knew where it was. Now they could calculate its speed and position against the background of stars, plot its approach, intercept it whenever they wanted, turn it from its course. It was what Vashlian had intended right from the beginning – and right from the beginning Eth had been involved.

It was clear to her now. She had been duped all along – a ten-year-old child coerced by Mistress Agla into becoming a dreamweaver, persuaded by Cable and Nemony into coming to the Academy, coerced again by Mistress Agla into staying there when she wanted to quit and flattered into taking part in Master Gerridon's experiment. They were conspirators, all of them. All of them conspiring with Vashlian to make use of her, even Cable. Cable, whom she had turned to and trusted, her acolyte now for almost seven years – he was one of them. His hands massaged her neck as he often did when she returned from a dream-walking session, seeking to ease the tension in her muscles, seeking to relax her. But she stiffened under his touch and he was bound to question.

"Are you all right, Eth?"

His concern was a sham and the hurt cut through her. A great anger filled her, flushed her cheeks and blazed in her eyes. And Master Gerridon stood before her, his inane grin at a job well done gradually fading. The room grew hushed. Dreamweavers and acolytes turned their heads to look.

"Are you all right?" Cable repeated.

And her anger exploded.

"I hate you!" screamed Eth. "And I hate you, too, Master Gerridon! I'll never work with any of you again!"

CHAPTER NINETEEN

Restored to consciousness several days earlier than scheduled due to an on-board emergency that was already over, Troy sat on the edge of the bed in his parents' cramped cabin and listened. Having done without the hour of physical and mental exercises, he still felt weak and shaky and somewhat confused. But the black coffee was a stimulant, as were Verity's words. His senses sharpened.

"*Eth* was *here*?" he said.

"Among a couple of dozen others," said Verity.

"Are you sure it was Eth?"

"She'd matured, of course, since we last saw her."

"That figures," muttered Troy.

"Lovely young ladies, all of them," murmured

Bill. "Dusky and delightful, with bright orange eyes, visions in thin air manifesting all over the ship. Two of them appeared in the engine room whilst I was there. Six or more in the cryogenic chamber. Others in the staff lounge and cargo holds."

"What did they want?" asked Troy.

"We haven't a clue," said Verity.

"They didn't stay long enough for us to ask them, more's the pity," said Bill. "Whoever gave the order to open fire has a lot to answer for."

"Al Cochrane," said Verity. "He made up his mind the moment we picked them up on the infra-red scanners and, at that point, how was I to know who they were?"

Troy frowned.

Old fears, old emotions re-awakened within him.

"It's always the same," he complained. "Shoot first and ask questions afterwards! And what's going to happen when we land? They'll be physical people then and how many will we slaughter?"

"None, if I can help it!" Verity said grimly.

"We've already arranged a meeting for tomorrow evening," Bill informed him. "All crew members, including you and the other junior personnel who have yet to be revived. We're going to discuss the whole issue of arms distribution and establish a few basic rules as to their use."

"Self-defence only," Verity said emphatically.

"And then only by trained crew members," said Bill.

"A select guard force," said Verity. "And all passengers to be barred from carrying weapons."

Suddenly Troy realised his parents meant what they said. They were not opposed to him at all. Not, as he had once believed, callous and indifferent to what went on but caring, honest people, compelled by a sense of justice to do whatever they could to ensure the safety of the inhabitants of the planet to which they were going. For the first time in his life he genuinely admired them, was glad to be related and glad to know them. Yet whatever they did, they would achieve nothing. Bill Morrison had no great standing. He was just a computer operator who would be redundant once they landed. And Verity was just one among a dozen or so other Flight Officers who probably wouldn't listen.

They wouldn't listen, thought Troy, and the use of weapons was not the issue. Armed or not, they were all invaders on someone else's world, people who had no right there. But after spending seven years travelling across space to settle on Arbroth, no amount of argument or reasoning would dissuade them from making a landfall. Already the ship was slowing down, preparing to switch off the warp-drive unit and enter the Roth Star's solar system. Already the full contingent of staff were being roused from their cryogenic sleep and restored to consciousness. In another few days they would be in orbit round the planet and in less than a week they would be landing.

And then, no matter what agreement Bill and Verity gained on the distribution of weapons, Arbroth would cease to belong to its native people. Three thousand thawed-out immigrants would divide it up between them. The dreams of F. J. Guttenham for a million-acre spread would become a reality. They would change the name of the Roth Star and call it the sun. Call Malroth the moon, re-christen Arbroth "New Earth" and begin to re-create the civilisation they had left behind. The ship carried all they needed. Its cargo holds were crammed with Portacabins, electrical generators, mining equipment, agricultural machinery, chemical apparatus, a microfilm library and the blueprints for heavy industry. Within a decade or so, oil refineries would grace the skyline, pipelines and pylons would stride across the landscape, processing plants and power stations would pour out their poisons. Within a century or so there would be airports and motorways and cities, and little would remain of the native way of life, their lands or their culture or their religious beliefs. Their children would be born into squalor and slavery and grow to be third-class citizens on another ruined world. But Troy's parents hoped and planned for something better, futile words that echoed in his head.

"It behoves us to try," Verity said firmly.

"Al Cochrane will take some persuading," muttered Bill.

"But the medics will support us."

"We'll need a democratic majority, Verity."

"I'm sure we can count on the others who were on our shift."

"Weapons mean power," said Bill. "And no one's going to relinquish them willingly."

"But we have to impose some kind of control," Verity insisted.

"I'm not disagreeing with you…"

"So if Troy goes to work on the younger members of the crew—"

"Not even Troy can create fifty human-rights enthusiasts in twenty-four hours, Verity. I still have a feeling that we're going to be out-voted."

"And if we are, what will we do?" asked Verity.

"Search me," sighed Bill.

"We can't just give up!"

Troy raised his head. "You could surreptitiously alter our course," he suggested.

The room fell silent. His parents stared at him.

"Would you care to elaborate on that?" asked his father.

"You could alter our course," said Troy. "Divert us elsewhere to some other planet. You've got access to the navigational computers and we don't *have* to go to Arbroth, do we? Or, failing that, you could sabotage the computers all together and prevent us landing."

"Don't be so damned ridiculous!" said Verity.

Outside, the crickets sang and rain dripped from the leaves of the creeper that twined around the balcony. Lake water lapped against the nearby shore. Music and jollity and the boom of Master Gerridon's laughter came drifting from the recreation block across the garden. Dreamweavers and acolytes were celebrating their success in finding the spaceship. But neither Eth nor Cable joined them. And the night sounds were unheard, drowned by their quarrel, the screech of her voice and Cable's heated replies.

"I knew nothing about it!"

"You must have!" Eth raged.

"How do you work that out?"

"Because you were the one who persuaded me to come here!"

"It wasn't just me!"

"Then you were in on it together! You *and* Nemony!"

"In on what?" Cable asked irritably.

"It's been a plot right from the beginning!" raged Eth. "It was why you were sent! You had to report on me – that's what you said! And you knew all the time what he was after! You knew what he wanted of me!"

"Who?" asked Cable.

"Vashlian!" said Eth.

Cable retaliated.

"I haven't seen Vashlian since… I hardly know the man! For crying out loud, Eth! He saved your life and your career! You'd have been dismissed from the Dreamweavers' Guild altogether if it hadn't been for him! And he told me nothing of where you'd been! Nothing of what had happened to you! If I cared about the future of Arbroth I was to bring you to the Academy, was all he said! He didn't say why! And I thought you agreed it wasn't a good idea for the spaceship to land? So what are you all screwed up about?"

"I've been used!" Eth said bitterly.

"Not by me!" Cable said emphatically. "I didn't know the purpose behind Master Gerridon's experiment. None of us did until you found the spaceship. Nor did I know that Vashlian was the

234

organiser!"

"So what does he intend to do?" Eth demanded.

"I don't know that either," snapped Cable.

"He must be planning something!"

"And what's it to you?" asked Cable. "You're out of it, aren't you? No longer responsible…"

"How can you say that?" screeched Eth. "Of course I'm responsible! I led Vashlian there in the first place, didn't I? And I was the one who relocated it! There are three thousand people on board that ship, Cable, and I'll be responsible for whatever happens to them, whatever Vashlian does!"

"Rubbish!" said Cable. "No one can be responsible for another person's actions. You surely haven't spent three years studying ethics without learning that?"

"You don't understand!" shrilled Eth.

"No," agreed Cable. "I don't understand! What goes on in you, Eth? Why are you so concerned about bunch of blasted aliens? Why should you care what happens to them or where they end up, as long as they don't land on Arbroth? We can't want them here, can we? It would be a sociological and ecological disaster. Vashlian is right to divert them! So why aren't you with us, Eth?"

She stared at him, silenced, not knowing what to say. And he waited for an explanation, waited and frowned. "Is there something you haven't told me?" he asked suspiciously. She turned away from him then, left the room and went to stand on the veranda, hoping the darkness would hide her. But Cable followed and he was not about to give up. His voice was accusing. "There is, isn't there? There *is* something you haven't told me!"

Eth leaned on the railing of the balcony and breathed in the scents of flowers that sweetened the night. Faint music faded. Dreamweavers and acolytes drifted, ghost-like, along the gravel path towards the housing block, ignoring her, all of them, as if her refusal to continue working with Master Gerridon made her some kind of traitor. She was exiled from their company. Between the trees the lake water rippled, red with Malroth's light, and among the stars was the ship in which Troy travelled. But in the flesh Eth would never meet him or welcome him to Arbroth.

"What's his name?" Cable asked curtly.

"Whose name?" she retorted.

"The boy with blue eyes," said Cable.

"I really don't know what you're talking about," said Eth.

"OK," said Cable. "Have it your way. But if you don't tell me, how can I help you? And how can I be expected to understand? And what's the point in my remaining your acolyte if you're not going to trust me? No point at all, is there, Eth? So I may as well go and get re-assigned and you can ask for someone else."

He limped along the veranda, and a sudden fear filled her. He was leaving her to live without him. For a boy with blue eyes she was about to lose the only friend she had, the last person who remained for her on Arbroth.

"His name's Troy!" Eth said loudly.

And Cable turned round.

The ship shifted out of warp-drive, winked into being among the distant reaches of the Roth Star's solar system and moved towards its final destination. Within it Troy lay on his bed in the cubby-hole cabin, staring up at the slats of the berth above him. It had been lowered from the wall to accommodate a junior commis chef named Winston Jessop, a black American restored fourteen hours ago from his cryogenic slumber.

Throughout their respective shifts there had been little chance of conversation or getting to know each other. Troy had been occupied with Dr Wynn-Stanley on the bio-check rounds and Jessop had been occupied in the kitchen, reconstituting and preparing dehydrated meals for a full contingency crew. And now Jessop slept, secure in the knowledge that, unlike on Earth, there would be no racial discrimination on the planet to which they were going. Weapons would be available to everyone, including himself.

Troy listened to his snores gradually growing quieter as his sleep deepened. Jessop did not know the meaning of racial discrimination, he thought bitterly, except when it applied to him. He had cast his vote to guarantee his own empowerment, not caring that another race of people would be used and abused as his ancestors had been. And his dream was no different from the dreams of F. J. Guttenham, although modified by his own lower expectations to a homestead by a river and a five-hundred acre farm. It was what he had been promised, he said, a new life, a new beginning, and no one was going to stop him, either on Arbroth or aboard this ship.

"Certainly not you, man," Jessop informed Troy.

Troy turned restlessly, out-voted, defeated, unable to sleep. He would land with the rest of them and there was nothing he, or his parents, or the medical contingent could do. It was up to Eth now, Eth and her people, simple people living simple lives – animal herders, fishermen, crofters and craftsmen – to fight for the world that was theirs. And would they? he wondered. Would they even realise they had to? And if they did, would they know how?

Dim blue light filled the cabin, peaceful and still. No sound within it but Jessop's regular breathing and the creak of the bed as Troy shifted his position, abandoned his thoughts and settled to sleep. His mind emptied, then filled with the eerie whispering of disincarnate voices, female voices speaking in a language he recognised but did not fully understand. And the words became images – images of himself and Jessop seen from another dimension and curled within their respective auras, cocoons of light, blue and orange, beautiful and shimmering but spoiled by filaments of darkness. And the voices continued – not dreamed or imagined, but there, in the cabin and linked to others in other cabins, unseen presences throughout the ship.

"Are they all sleeping?"

"All but one."

"And he's not aware of us."

"Leave him out of it then."

"How many do we have in these rooms all together?"

"Well over a hundred."

"One for each of us."

"And the rest are on duty elsewhere."

"Shall we begin?"

"Wait for the first rapid eye movement."

"Gently to begin with…"

"And keep in unison."

"The others will be open to us the moment they begin to dream."

"Here we go…"

The voices and images faded and Troy waited. Minutes ticked by and nothing happened. Maybe he had imagined after all, he thought. He turned his head, silently, in order to see – and there was no one there, no one in the cabin apart from Jessop and himself. The bed-slats creaked in the bunk above him as Jessop moved, thrashed in the throes of a dream or a nightmare, moaned and muttered and ground his teeth. Then, suddenly, he awoke with a bloodcurdling scream, leapt from the bunk and cowered in the corner of the room, babbling with terror.

Troy sat up and reached for the light switch.

The fear remained on Jessop's face, and his eyes rolled wildly.

"What's wrong?" asked Troy. "What the hell is it?"

"Oh God!" wailed Jessop. "You don't know what's waiting on that planet! You don't know what we're going to! Ain't no gun going to kill a thing like that!"

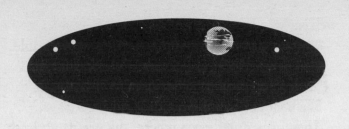

CHAPTER TWENTY

Eth fixed her eyes on the stars.

"There's a link," she said. "Some kind of bond between us. I don't understand what it is, but I know it exists, and it never has been accidental. There's a reason behind it – and what happens to him matters."

"Only to you," said Cable.

"No," said Eth. "Not just to me. It matters to everyone. It's representative, isn't it? Representative of everyone who lives on this planet, including you. If we harm those people, if we damage them in any way, then we also damage ourselves and Arbroth, because our emotions and our actions not only affect our own personal auras, but the aura of our planet as well."

"And presumably so will theirs," retorted Cable.

"So maybe we can heal them?" Eth argued.

"As you healed Liadd?" asked Cable.

She bent her head.

There was quiet everywhere, the pre-dawn hush when even the frogs and insects slept. But the dreamweavers and their acolytes were not sleeping. Even from the physical dimension Eth could sense them... threads of existences strung out across the ether. She wanted to go, wanted to join them, find out what they were doing, but all night long Cable had kept her talking, defeated her on every tack she took. Now he reminded her of Liadd and her own failure. That kind of psychic contamination would require decades of treatment, Vashlian had said.

"They *can't* come here," Cable insisted.

And Eth had run out of arguments.

She sat in silence, watched as the first sudden streaks of dawn began to disperse the darkness and dim the stars, pink light picking out the shapes of things, glinting on the lawn grass and the rain-soaked trees. One by one the birds awoke and sang. One by one the first group of dreamweavers returned to their beds and their bodies and the second group departed. Finally, wearily, in order to escape to her own bed and follow them, Eth was bound to agree. Vashlian was right; Cable was right: the aliens could not land on Arbroth, not even Troy.

"But what we do to prevent them, and what happens to them, still matters," she declared.

"I imagine Vashlian is aware of that," Cable replied.

"So what is he up to?" Eth inquired. "What new experiment is Master Gerridon conducting now?"

Cable yawned and shrugged.

"There's only one way to find that out," he said.

He meant ask, thought Eth. And who would tell her? Not Vashlian himself, even if she could find him, nor Master Gerridon either. She no longer figured in the scheme of things. She was outcast by her own refusal to participate and regarded as a traitor by everyone who knew her. And, damned by association, no one would tell Cable either.

"So how do I find out?" Eth demanded.

"Go to the ship," said Cable. "See for yourself."

She turned her head to stare at him. How had he known that was what she planned? But he was not looking at her. He was gazing at the lake beyond the trees, rose-pink water rippling in the sunrise. Pale light gleamed on the smooth dome of his skull, glinted gold in the nose stud he was wearing.

"Are you actually suggesting…?"

"It's logical, isn't it?" said Cable.

"And you'd stay linked to me?"

"If I don't there's no deal."

"I could warn them," said Eth. "I could try and counteract—"

"That's up to you," said Cable.

"So why help me?" asked Eth. "Why make yourself an accomplice to whatever I decide to do? Why, Cable?"

He glanced at her then.

His tawny eyes were as expressionless as his face.

"I'm your acolyte," he said. "It's part of my job to go along with you. I may not agree with you, but I have to allow that you might be right. Maybe it does matter what happens to those people. And it certainly matters to you what happens to Troy. So go to him, Eth, if that's what you want. Go and find out what he means to you and what you mean to yourself. Go and find out where your responsibilities truly lie." He yawned again and rose to his feet. "I'm going to bed," he said. "Let me know when you're ready to depart."

The nightmares had begun the moment *Exodus* entered the Roth Star's solar system – a common dream, a shared terror – and no one was immune except for the three thousand emigrants in the cryogenic chamber. The effects on the crew were immediate and devastating. Twenty-four hours of sleep deprivation caused nerves and tempers to fray, a kind of growing madness in every person in every department, even in Troy. He had only to doze off for more than a few seconds and the nightmare would begin again – the black pyramids of Arbroth crackling with infernal power. He did not need to re-experience the rest. The preliminary images were, in themselves, enough to wake him in a pool of sweat. And when the fear abated and his heart stopped hammering, he was afraid to sleep again – everyone was.

Stimulants issued by the medical department kept them alert and functioning but could not keep them awake indefinitely. There was a rash of emotional breakdowns, quarrels, arguments, a lack of communication, a loss of self-control and a marked increase in aggressive behaviour. A fight broke out in the kitchen quarters. Jessop clouted the head chef with a saucepan and had to be returned to the cryogenic chamber. And others, on the medics' advice, accepted the same release.

Troy began to long for it – theta sleep, a sleep too deep for dreams. And being off-duty was the worst time. Then he had nothing to concentrate on, nothing to occupy his mind and stave off the need to sleep. Five minutes in the staff lounge watching a video and his eyelids began to grow heavy and he had to fight against the lassitude that threatened to take him over, request another pill to stave off the terror of the nightmare that would inevitably happen the moment he allowed himself to succumb.

Jack Wynn-Stanley shook his head.

"No can do, Troy, not any more. We're running short of stimulants and I have my orders. Essential personnel only. And you're not on the list."

"So how am I supposed to combat it?"

"Do you want to go back to your cryogenic berth?"

Sweet oblivion – sleep without dreams, without knowing. Finally faced with it, Troy frowned. He was exhausted, as was everyone else who remained awake, the medic, too, grey-faced and haggard with dark circles ringing his eyes. But something prompted him to stay awake, something at the back of his mind told him it was important.

"Thanks but no thanks," he decided.

"They *are* only dreams," Jack Wynn-Stanley reminded him.

Only dreams, thought Troy, as he raided the coffee machine and went to his cabin. And was it coincidence that everyone dreamed the same? It happened sometimes within closed communities, the medics had claimed. But this was a recurring nightmare and it seemed to have purpose – teaching them to fear the planet to which they were heading, making them dread the very idea of landing there. Hard-headed, rational men and women woke up screaming, and Verity shuddered at the mere mention of the word "Arbroth".

Only dreams… but it could almost be a form of aversion therapy, thought Troy. Several times, on the brink of sleep, he had heard voices, female voices whispering around him. He had not reported them, but others had. They were auditory hallucinations, the medics had explained, the mind playing tricks and yet another symptom of sleep deprivation. But what if they were real? thought Troy. People whispering in another dimension? Girls like Eth who could leave their physical bodies? Girls with psychic powers deliberately transmitting a series of diabolical images? No, he decided, Eth would not do that. Visions like that were beyond her. There was no horned God where she came from, no goat-legged Satan, no Devil emanating evil and feeding on human souls. Those images came from Earth, something Eth could not even conceive of, and, if she were typical, nor could anyone else of her kind. Apart from her brother, perhaps? Her brother might.

He dismissed that thought. They were definitely

girls he had heard and he heard them again now – girls whispering in his cabin, siren voices, soft and soothing, lulling away his fear. Sleep sucked at his mind. Dream images formed in a few seconds of darkness and coffee spilled down his shirt front as he jerked himself awake.

"I'll take this one," said Eth.

And the whisperers responded.

"What are you doing here, Eth?"

"I've come to join you."

"Master Gerridon told us you weren't to—"

"I apologised, and he changed his mind."

"You know the images we have to weave?"

"Obviously I know."

"And the emotions we have to transmit?"

"Those too."

"The moment they sleep, the moment they begin to dream…"

"I'll take this one," she repeated.

"He isn't asleep yet."

"Then I'll wait until he is."

"I'm glad you're with us again, Eth!"

"Yes," murmured Eth. "I'm glad, too."

The whispering ceased. There was a moment of silence… silence and a sense of presence. She was still there, thought Troy, somewhere in the dim blue shadows around him.

"Eth?"

Almost immediately she manifested beside his bed.

"Be quiet!" she hissed.

"What are—?"

She held a finger to her lips, and her voice murmured urgently in his head.

"Wait until they've gone. Wait until they're occupied elsewhere. I don't want them to overhear what we say."

He stared at her, a ghost girl with dusky skin, black braided hair and tangerine eyes gazing into nothingness, listening and waiting. She was older than he remembered, a young woman, grown as he had slept. She had appeared before, Verity had told him, forty-eight hours or so ago, she and a couple of dozen others. They had vanished when Al Cochrane gave the order to open fire. And a little over twelve hours later the nightmares had begun.

Tired as he was, Troy was still capable of rational thinking. Things were beginning to add up, and it was not as the medics claimed at all. What was happening on board the ship was no natural phenomenon. They were being fed those nightmares, quite deliberately. A garbled cry came from the adjoining cabin and Eth swung to face him.

"I came to tell you—"

249

"I already know," said Troy.

"I suppose you're bound to," she said wretchedly.

"Are they friends of yours?"

"Not any more," she said.

"So who are they?" Troy asked curiously.

"Dreamweavers," she told him. "Students from the Academy. They're working for Vashlian and Master Gerridon and they've been specially trained. They're trying to prevent you from landing on Arbroth."

Troy leaned back against the pillows. It all made sense to him now. They were fighting for their world in the only way they could, dreamweavers, specially trained for the occasion, weaving them nightmares, filling Troy and the whole crew with irrational fear. It was a brilliant idea, psychological warfare and no way to counter it. Troy wanted to applaud Vashlian or Master Gerridon, whichever one of them had dreamed up the plan. He wanted to laugh for what he himself had become, a victim of the very thing he had hoped for, the battle for Arbroth that Eth and her kind were going to win. But something stopped him – the look in her eyes and the expression on her face, the transmission of her distress.

"It was my fault," she said miserably.

"How do you mean?" Troy asked her.

"I led them here," she said.

"So don't let it worry you," said Troy. "I *do* understand. And what's a few nightmares between friends?"

Relief showed in her tangerine eyes.

"There could be a way to foil them," she informed him. "If you have chemicals on board I can tell you how to grow sleep crystals."

"What?" said Troy.

"Sleep crystals," said Eth. "They affect the patterns of your brainwaves and you sleep too deeply for dreaming. In the right mulch they will grow overnight, like mushrooms, and protect you from nightmares until you land."

"Land?" asked Troy. "What are you talking about? That's the last thing you want, for Christ's sake! I appreciate the offer, Eth, but I'd rather you didn't tell me. Now I know the purpose I prefer to bear it, or not as the case may be." She stared at him, not understanding, and he smiled at her bewilderment. "Your dreamweavers are doing fine," he told her. "Give us another forty-eight hours and we'll be ready to throw in the sponge, get the hell out of this solar system and never come back."

Disbelief showed on Eth's face. "What are you saying?" she asked.

"Do you want it in images?"

"You surely can't mean—?"

"I wouldn't say it if I didn't mean it," Troy assured her.

"What about us?" she asked him.

"Us?" said Troy.

"You and me," said Eth. "And the bond that is between us."

"What's that got to do with it?" asked Troy.

"If you care about me…"

"*If?*" said Troy. "What do you mean by *if*, Eth? Isn't it obvious that I care about you? Why else would I be willing…?"

She looked at him, puzzled.

"But I thought you said you didn't want to land on Arbroth? That you hoped our dreamweavers would drive you away? That you don't mind if we never meet…"

"But that doesn't mean – oh, I get it."

It was Troy's turn to stare at her – her orange eyes, the sheen on her hair. She was beautiful, he thought, transparent and beautiful. And yes, he wanted to land on her planet, wanted to meet her, wanted it more than he had ever wanted anything in his whole life and so did she. It was for him she had come here, a girl with her own dreams, willing to betray her kind in her effort to help him, wanting the ship to land no matter what the consequences might be.

She did not have a clue, he realised, no idea what

those on board this ship would do, no idea of the effect they would have. It was beyond her conception. In loving him she would gladly welcome all of them to Arbroth, welcome the destruction of her world and all her race. But he, if he loved her, could not let her do that. No matter what it took, no matter what hurt he inflicted on her, he could not let her do it. He shook his head.

"Sorry, Eth, but whatever it is that's between us is irrelevant in this. Remember what you once said of us? We're damaged and dangerous – and that's the truth. We've already ruined our own planet and why should we be allowed to ruin yours? Vashlian is right! Master Gerridon is right! They're right, whoever they are, believe you me! So go and join them, Eth. Go and join them and forget about us."

"But what they're doing is wrong!" she protested.

"How d'you work that out?" asked Troy.

"It's psychological torture!" said Eth.

Troy laughed mockingly. "It'll be more than psychological torture we'll inflict on you if we're allowed to land!" he informed her. "But if you don't have the stomach for it, then keep yourself out of it and leave it to those who do! Let the dreamweavers drive us elsewhere! There are millions of other planets in this galaxy, millions of other worlds we can land on and despoil. We'll find somewhere else."

"And you and I will never meet!" she wailed.

Troy shrugged.

"So what?" he repeated. "It's no big deal, is it? All I'll be missing out on is a few screws."

The image formed in his mind, was received and understood. Bright tears welled and shimmered in Eth's eyes and Troy's own feelings tore at him. She had been a part of his life, a part of his dreams, growing towards him for seven long years, and he did not want leave her this way. He wanted to leave it lovely between them. He wanted her to know he had never cared for anyone as he cared for her. But he could not afford to be swayed. His voice stayed mocking.

"Go home, Eth. Go home where you belong. What's between you and me doesn't really mean very much and I'm not a particularly nice person. I'm not worth hanging around for, not worth the grief. There's a girl on board called Hannah Guttenham and I kind of promised her... You'd better shove off before she gets here. Go and latch onto someone else."

He settled back against the pillows and closed his eyes. He did not want to see her face or know what he had done to her. He needed to sleep now, needed the nightmares to wash away the memory, a dose of fear to erase the anguish and heal the pain.

"I'll give your regards to my mother," he said.
But Eth was no longer there.

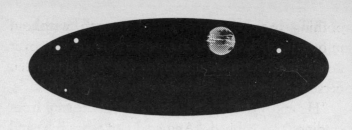

CHAPTER TWENTY-ONE

Eth had left when the Roth Star was at its zenith,
followed the group of dreamweavers to the ship. She
had gone there for Troy, wanting to help him,
wanting to warn him, but he had cast scorn on her
motives, mocked her for her stupidity and driven her
away. Go home, he had told her, go home to where
you belong. And she returned to her room at the
onset of twilight, lay face down on the bed and wept.

"What happened?" asked Cable. "Did you find
him? Did you speak to him? Did they shoot at you
again? You weren't transmitting so I wasn't able—
What happened, Eth?"

She tried to tell him, tried to explain, words being
blurted out between bouts of sobbing. She held

nothing back. She had no reason to withhold information from Cable, not any more. It was over now, over and done with, everything ended between herself and Troy.

"He said Vashlian is right to prevent the ship from landing!" she sobbed. "And he doesn't care if he and I never meet in this dimension! That the bond between us is just a sexual thing!"

"Are you sure?" asked Cable. "Are you sure that's what he said?"

"I'm telling you, aren't I?" sobbed Eth.

Cable laughed. "Well, flip me! Who would have thought it?"

"It's nothing to laugh at!" wept Eth.

"But it's wonderful!" chuckled Cable. "And so's he!"

Eth pounded the pillow with her fists. "How can you say that, Cable! How would you feel if someone said it about you and me? It's an insult! An insult on me and on our whole society!"

"Oh come off it," said Cable. "Sexual attraction is a fact of life, even on Arbroth, and it often gets mistaken for love."

"I'm aware of that!" Eth said angrily. "And I wouldn't mind if it was true! But it isn't – and Troy knows it! So why did he say it? Why did he deny—?"

"Isn't it obvious?" asked Cable.

"No!" said Eth. "What reason can there be for deliberately hurting someone? What reason for cheapening the love that exists between one person and another! It's a despicable thing to do!"

"He *is* an alien," Cable reminded her. "And what kind of people do you think his are, Eth, with their damaged auras and their dangerous weapons? What kind of world did they come from and why did they leave it? For the same reason we left Malroth centuries ago? Think about it, Eth. What self-recognition led Troy to admit that Vashlian is right?"

The questions hung in the air. Eth did not want to consider them, but the answers were there in her mind. They were hateful people, all of them, as damaged and dangerous as Liadd, as corrupt as their auras. Even Troy. He was no different, Vashlian had told her. And Troy had admitted Vashlian was right. He was not a very nice person, he had said, and they had already ruined the planet they came from and could not be allowed to ruin another. Fresh tears trickled down Eth's cheeks.

"I wish I'd never gone to the ship!" she wept.

"How can you wish that?" Cable demanded.

"Do you really need to ask?"

"You can't go on living with illusions, Eth."

"I still can't believe that's all it was!" sobbed Eth. "The link between Troy and me was more than just sexual attraction. I know it was and so did he!"

Cable sighed. "You're just not seeing it, are you? You can be totally and absolutely correct and it doesn't matter one iota because Troy has chosen to deny it. He's denied it, and it's over, and you have to accept it. You have to accept it, Eth."

She chewed her lip. She had to accept the lesson of her own experience that Cable had set up for her.

Go there, he had told her.

Go to the ship and seek Troy out.

Find out what he means to you.

Cable had not cared, either, how much she was hurt. He had laughed when she told him what had happened, laughed as she had cried. It was what he had wanted, what he had hoped for, but the end of everything as far as she was concerned. She raised her head to look at him but she could not see his face. He stood with his back to her in the open doorway, a silhouette against the sunset beyond. He was her acolyte, bound to her for as long as she remained bound to the Dreamweavers' Guild, her continued well-being his only concern. But he had betrayed her along with everyone else.

"You've been against me right from the start!" Eth said accusingly. "Hand-in-glove with Vashlian and Mistress Agla—"

"Don't start that again!" Cable said wearily.

"But it's true!" said Eth.

"How can it be when there aren't any sides?"

"But you must be very pleased!" Eth said bitterly.

"Pleased about what?" asked Cable.

"With the way things have turned out!"

"It's not over yet," said Cable.

"It is between Troy and me!"

Cable turned to regard her. Lamplight from within the room winked on his nose stud. His eyes narrowed thoughtfully.

"Is that all you can think of, Eth? Your own little life? And what about Arbroth? What about the future of our planet? That ship could still land here in spite of all Vashlian's efforts. And even Troy cares more than you do! At least he's *with* us. For Arbroth and for us, he did what he had to – lied to you and drove you away, turned traitor to his own people, sacrificed himself and them to spare us from invasion. But what have you done, Eth? And where are you that you think we're all against you? Aren't you one of us? Aren't you a part of this world?"

She stared at him and he turned his back on her – a young man, lame in one leg, leaning on the balcony rail in the gathering darkness. And was it true, what he had said? she wondered. Had Troy lied to her? Spurned her for the sake of Arbroth? For a world that was not his own? Did he believe, as Vashlian and

Cable and everyone else seemed to believe, that its future was more important than truth or honesty or anyone's personal happiness? More important even than Troy's own life? Could Arbroth really be worth so much to him that he was willing to accept all the nightmares the dreamweavers wove and the suffering they inflicted, risk the safety of the ship, smash the hopes and dreams of the three thousand people on board, and destroy what existed between Eth and himself? It had never occurred to her that his concern for her planet could be greater than his love for her. It had never occurred to her that was how Cable felt, too, and everyone else she knew.

The planet moved through her memory – Arbroth, green and brown, with lakes and forests and mountains. She had stood on the auric plain and viewed its halo, a rainbow glory, iridescent with life and light. And who was she to place herself above it? Who was she to think her own life, dreams and happiness, and her private love for an alien boy, were more important than the well-being of a world?

With a quick flush of shame Eth realised that they had been telling her that all along, all of them in their various ways – Vashlian, Mistress Agla, Cable and Troy. And how many times had Nemony advised her not to get personally involved? Advised her never to act from her emotions? She had known from the beginning that the life and work of a dreamweaver was not for her own self-aggrandisement but for the good of everyone and the good of the world.

Too young, everyone had said of her. Too young to know the meaning of responsibility. But they had made use of her talents in spite of her until, finally, she learned that it was not other people who had gone against her, but she who had gone against herself. In everything personal she had failed. And now she was free, free of all the relationships that bound her, her own dreams, her own desires, her own wishes. All that remained was a potential dreamweaver, the powers she possessed and a love that was greater than personal affections – and if she denied that then she denied herself.

It still mattered what happened to Troy and people on board the alien spaceship, but not for the reasons she had thought. It mattered as much as her family mattered, exiled on Malroth. They were human beings, all of them, and although she accepted now that they could not live on Arbroth, they still had a right to life, to all the help and caring she, or Vashlian, or anyone else could give them.

She rose from the bed and went to stand beside Cable on the balcony. The darkness was complete now, Malroth hanging low above the lake, its orange–red light reflecting on the water, and tropical stars shining clear and bright. Somewhere up there was an alien spaceship and a group of dreamweavers under Vashlian's command who did what they had to. He was a visionary, Cable had said, a man who worked among the exiled people on Malroth, who used the Dreamweavers' Guild and used Eth, too, to make his vision a reality.

She might have hated Vashlian once, but hatred was an emotion she could no longer own, and anyway she had seen his aura – the glowing purple aura of one who was wiser and greater than she. She did not fully understand him – a man who could hold a knife at Liadd's throat yet work to heal him – but she needed to. And she needed to know what happened to Troy and Verity, too, how Arlynn and Hurli were and how Kanderin fared.

She touched Cable's hand.

"I'm sorry," she murmured.

"For what?" he asked.

"For everything," said Eth. "But most of all for not trusting you."

Cable put his arm round her shoulders and hugged her to him.

"Welcome home," he said.

But he was wrong, thought Eth, and so had Troy been wrong. Her home was not here on Arbroth. To Arbroth she had given all she had to give – her childhood, her girlhood, seventeen years of her life, her love for Troy as the final sacrifice. It could ask no more of her. The house where she had been born was closed and shuttered and the village had Nemony for its dreamweaver and would not need her. And all over the planet's surface she had roamed with the groups of students, but nowhere had she seen a place she wished to work and settle, nowhere had she found a place that felt like home.

I want to go home... I want to go home... the chant of a homesick child echoed in her memory and the red sands of Malroth whirled through her mind. It's a powerful bond that draws a dreamweaver to her place, Vashlian had said. And it was as if he had seen her future from the very beginning.

"How would you feel about going to Malroth?" she asked Cable.

Unshaven men, women with unkempt hair, struggled to keep a grip on their reason and make the last few final decisions. There were not many left, no more than a couple of dozen who had resisted the lure of the cryogenic chamber. And the planet lay ahead of them, a green-brown world, beautiful and alluring among swirls of white cloud. The scanners showed it in close-up – its farms, fields and forests, its lakes reflecting the sunlight, the snow shining on the peaks of its mountains and over the gleaming expanse of its northern ice-cap.

"It looks very innocent, doesn't it?" Troy said slyly.

"Shut it!" Al Cochrane replied.

"Don't start blaming Troy!" Verity said sharply. "It's not his fault this ship is being invaded."

"It was his association that led them here!"

"Do we know that for certain?" asked Verity.

"We don't even know for certain that we *are* being invaded," said Jack Wynn-Stanley. "Nothing shows on the scanners and there are other possible explanations."

"Mass hallucinations!" Al Cochrane snarled. "Tell that to the marines! They're here! And we all know it!"

"So what do we do?" asked Verity.

Their approach trajectory took them between the two planets. Malroth, a red desert world of rocks and sand, barren and uninviting, was a place to be ignored but, even as they crossed the dividing line between day and night, the scanners continued to pan the surface of Arbroth. Minute pin-pricks of light indicated the main inhabited areas with huge expanses of darkness in between. As Troy had said, it was all very innocent. Nothing to remind them of their nightmares or re-instil their terror of landing there. Seated at the navigational computer, Bill Morrison turned his head.

"Do I take us into orbit?" he asked.

"No!" said Troy.

"Shut it!" Al Cochrane said again.

"They *are* only dreams," Jack Wynn-Stanley insisted for the umpteenth time. "Visions from our own collective unconscious rooted in the religious mythology of Earth and nothing to do with Arbroth."

"And according to our technological read-outs there is no power source there," Ellis Hargreaves added. "Those black pyramids are as harmless as the pyramids of Egypt. Inert obsidian, even if they are hollow."

"So do I take us into orbit?" Bill repeated.

"You know my feelings," Verity said curtly.

"We're being warned-off," agreed Troy.

Al Cochrane turned. His lean face was grey from lack of sleep. There was an edge of hysteria in his voice.

"You want to spend the rest of your lives trekking around the universe looking for a place to land? We could be old or dead before that happens! The cryogenics aren't built to last indefinitely and nor do we have the means to produce our own supply of oxygen! We've got no choice, Verity! And I'm not being driven away by a horde of invisible wenches and a few flaming nightmares! Take us into orbit, Bill. We'll head for the sunrise and the first available landfall."

The decision was made. Troy's father nodded and turned to the computer.

And the nightmare began.

The electrics dimmed. The instruments went crazy. Needles whirled round their dials. The navigational display units fuzzed and flickered. Only the vision screens remained operative, showing the planet below cobwebbed with power. It was happening just as they had dreamed it. Clouds swirled above its surface and the black pyramids were not inert at all. Crackles of light joined one to another, criss-crossing the darkness. The clouds boiled and seethed and coalesced. And a face formed within them, horned and hideous and terrifyingly familiar.

Nancy Kwang screamed and covered her eyes.

Al Cochrane's face grew pale as ash.

And Bill cried out: "We're losing control of the ship!"

"God help us!" moaned Verity.

But it was nothing to do with God, thought Troy. It was just a group of dreamweavers doing what they had to, weaving their images, influencing matter with their minds. And *Exodus* turned in response to them. Weightless in the vacuum of space, she swung from her set trajectory to resume her journey on a different course towards a different destination.

"Do something to counter it!" Al Cochrane howled.

Troy smiled as the jets failed to fire.

Arbroth fled from the vision screens.

And the air around him was full of presences.

"Say goodbye to Eth for me!" he said loudly.

CHAPTER TWENTY-TWO

Mistress Agla clasped Eth's hands.

"You will not find it easy," she warned. "Malroth is a hard place and they are hard people who live there. They do not take kindly to anyone associated with the Dreamweavers' Guild. It is we who judged them unfit to live on Arbroth and sent them into exile. So do not expect them to welcome you, not even your own family."

"I won't," Eth promised.

"Nor Vashlian either," the old woman added.

"The Administrators have already told me," Eth informed her. "Our connection with Vashlian is never official. And if we need to contact him we must do so only through the etheric plane."

Mistress Agla nodded. "It is important that you understand," she said.

In the last two days, since Eth had made her application for transfer and taken her vows, she had come to understand many things. The Dreamweavers' Guild, apart from the worthwhile work it did, was also a filtering system. Not only the likes of Liadd were removed from circulation but others too. Anyone who publicly questioned the established way of life, or whose scientific or technological inventiveness, if applied, could upset the balance of nature or disturb the existing order, were sent to various academies to be tutored.

They were tutored, as the dreamweavers themselves were tutored, to direct their minds and their lives towards the good of the planet and its people, and exile to Malroth awaited the few who refused to comply. Just in time Eth had abandoned her own little rebellion. But she would never forget the three thousand souls on board the space ship who were denied a landing. Nor would she ever escape from the ties of her past, the damage her race had done on Malroth and the banished people who lived there. Arlynn and Hurli, Liadd and her mother – they mattered to her still, in spite of what they had done.

"Take care of yourself," Mistress Agla murmured.

"Cable will do that," Eth said firmly. "And remember me to Nemony when next you see her."

Withdrawing her hands from the old woman's grasp, Eth gathered up skirts of her new black gown and turned towards the trans-matt terminal where Cable was waiting.

"Are you quite sure about this?" he asked.

"Yes," she replied. For herself she *was* sure, but she was still unsure about him. "You don't *have* come with me," she informed him.

Cable raised a quizzical eyebrow. "Don't I?" he said.

"Malroth is worse than the swamps or the tundra, and you're not bound."

"I'm your acolyte," he said stoutly.

"I could dismiss you," she offered.

"As Troy dismissed you?" he asked. "Sorry, Eth, but that won't work. I go where you go and nothing will ever change that."

She laughed then, picked up her travel bag and stepped inside the terminal. The door slid closed against the grounds of the Academy and the old adjudicator who had willed her there. Arbroth fled in a white vortex of light. And probably, as Vashlian had done, Mistress Agla had known all along the price Eth would pay for a green–brown world and a way of life that damaged no one.

The exit trans-matt was cramped and small, its walls empty of grid maps and information. And the door opened into an underground room, letting fall a shaft of brightness on a dusty floor that faded into the absolute darkness beyond it.

"Can this be right?" asked Eth.

"It has to be," said Cable. "They were the right co-ordinates."

He dragged out their bags and, reluctantly, she followed him, her new black gown brushing dust from the stones. The cold was intense and there was no one to greet them. No sign of life apart from themselves, no trace of light beyond the darkness that confronted them, no sound but their own breathing. Then, as the door to the trans-matt slid shut, a distant door opened and someone carrying a lantern came hurrying towards them.

She was a woman in long skirts, her dark hair coiled round her head in a tangled plait, her bare arms wrapped by a tattered shawl. "Sorry to keep you waiting," she said politely. "I was feeding the baby and everyone else is—Eth? Is that you, Eth?" Arlynn swung the lantern closer. "It is!" she said, laughingly. "It *is* you! You've come to join us... and Cable, too. Oh Eth – this is wonderful!"

Impulsively, still holding the lantern, Arlynn

caught Eth's hand and kissed her cheek, then went to Cable and kissed him too. Her orange eyes shone in the lamplight as, once again, she turned her attention to her sister.

"Wait until Hurli sees you!" she exclaimed. "Wait until I tell him! They said you had not died but we didn't know you had recovered! It was worth it then, worth what he did. He'll be glad about that."

Eth gazed at her in bewilderment. "I thought you would both hate me," she murmured.

Arlynn chuckled. "Why ever should we hate you, Eth?"

"It's my fault you're here," Eth told her. "I wove the dream that drove Hurli—"

"You wove the dream that gave him back to me," Arlynn contradicted. "He told me of it, Eth. It made him realise what Liadd was really like. And what good does it do to throw the blame on someone else? What's the point in ending up bitter and hating? As vicious and twisted as Aldo and Liadd? They're bandits, Eth, and the ones who follow them. They kill, and rob, and rape, and murder! It's everyone's choice, Mistress Meera said. We can either go and join them and live as they do, which is what our mother chose to do – or we can..." Arlynn frowned and shook her head. "Me and Hurli are not like them!" she said fiercely. Then she smiled again. "It's too cold to stay here talking. Come upstairs into the sunlight. Come and meet Mistress Meera and my little Sorren."

Eth picked up her travel bag and, with Cable behind her, followed Arlynn into the cavernous darkness. Their footsteps on the floor were muffled by the dust and their voices echoed.

"You and Hurli have a child?" Eth asked.

"She has eight teeth now and has taken her first steps," Arlynn said proudly. "Because of Sorren, and what's recently happened here, we could have had our exile rescinded and returned to Arbroth. Most of the exiles were given the opportunity – except for the likes of Aldo and Liadd, and the women who serve them. Mistress Meera urged us to go. But we've worked hard on Malroth, me and Hurli. It's home to us now and we won't give it up, not for anyone! And sometimes I sense something binds us here, although I don't know what."

"As a race we have our roots here," said Eth.

"Anyway," said Arlynn, "someone has to stay and teach the rudiments of survival, and I keep hoping Kanderin will come to her senses and join us. Maybe you'll be able to help her, Eth? Dreamweave for her as you once did for Hurli? We need all the dreamweavers we can get on Malroth now. Are you the only one the Academy sent? Or are there others set to follow? We can't keep the trans-matt open much longer. It will soon have to be immobilised, Mistress Meera says."

Still chattering, Arlynn and the lantern preceded Eth and Cable along an underground corridor. Their shadows danced on smooth stone walls, and deeper darknesses loomed through empty doorways into countless other rooms. It was part of a ruined city, Arlynn informed them, bigger by far than any town on Arbroth and mostly buried by sand. They were in the basement of some great building where Mistress Meera and some of the exiles had made their homes.

"You mean you actually live with a dreamweaver?" asked Eth.

"Meera isn't like Nemony," Arlynn explained. "None of the dreamweavers are who live on Malroth. They're not set apart from us, and they don't judge us or try to impose their ideas. On Malroth we've got nothing to live up to, have we? No set community standards. We are just people who are forced to live and work together in order to survive. And if we can't do that then the only alternative is to abandon any attempt at morality and join the bandits."

"Do they really commit rape and murder?" asked Cable.

"They have done," said Arlynn. "And among themselves they probably still do. According to

Meera, bandits belong to a different social order all together, human parasites living from the efforts of others, their consciences over-ruled by their struggle for supremacy. Sometimes, when I think of them, I fear for Kanderin's life…"

"But not for your own?" asked Cable.

"Not since Vashlian became their leader," said Arlynn.

"Vashlian?" said Eth. "Vashlian is a bandit?"

Arlynn glanced at her.

"Does that surprise you?" she asked. "Don't you remember when he came to our house posing as Mistress Agla's acolyte and held a knife to Liadd's throat? He obviously became violent enough to get himself exiled, and violent enough to take command from Aldo, too."

Eth frowned. Somehow she could not believe that of Vashlian. He was hard and ruthless, certainly. Surely he had to be if he lived and worked with men such as Aldo and Liadd? And merely surviving on Malroth would make any person hard. Arlynn herself displayed a grit and determination she had never possessed on Arbroth. But Vashlian had powers that could counteract and deflect physical violence, and he had not been exiled but was here for the same reason Eth was here – because he chose to be.

"How do you know Vashlian took command by using violence?" Cable inquired.

Arlynn shrugged. "I don't," she admitted. "It happened before me and Hurli came here. I simply assumed. But he's made a difference, Mistress Meera says. The bandits may continue to raid our settlements and steal our food, but at least no one's been killed and no woman's been dragged away for their sexual enjoyment since Vashlian's been in charge. We're given time to hide these days, and sometimes we even have time to salvage most of our supplies. I don't know how, but Meera says the dreamweavers receive warning of each pending attack."

Eth glanced at Cable. Both of them guessed how the dreamweavers received warning. If Vashlian could dream-walk, he could likely weave dreams as well. It was a dangerous game he played. Nor was it only Arbroth he worked to protect, but the exiles on Malroth, too. And by taking command of the bandits he was also protecting Liadd and Aldo, and others like them, from the worst excesses of their natures. Eth's respect for him grew. And had he done something to ensure the survival of those aboard the alien spaceship, it would have been complete. But he had denied Troy and his people a landfall and that troubled her still. Frowning to herself in an effort to understand the man, she followed Arlynn up a flight of worn stone steps.

"Things will be changing on Malroth for all of us now," Arlynn announced, "the bandits included. They are likely to be receiving a dose of their own medicine, be attacked and enslaved themselves if they do not guard against it. But you know about that, of course. "

"Know about what?" asked Eth.

"Surely it's why you've come here?" Arlynn replied.

She opened a door at the top and Eth blinked in the sudden light. The room was more vast than any Council Hall on Arbroth – a kitchen-cum-workshop with a chipped mosaic floor, smelling of dried fish and cheeses and new baked bread. A kiln and cooking oven stood at one end, stone sinks and dyeing vats at the other. Stretched shote-skins pinned to the wall behind her concealed the door through which she had entered, and work-benches were everywhere with the muddles of making things – eel pots and fishing creels, spades, hoes and hay forks, clay storage jars and the stacked tools needed for survival.

Eth saw it all in a single glance and the baby, too, sleeping in a basket-weave crib. Yet she saw none of it. Her gaze fixed on the unglazed windows before her and the open arch of the door, on the clear brilliance of the sunlight and the scene outside. The wind whispered, blowing eddies of dust across a stretch of red sand. To the left and right small walled fields clung to the edges of the marsh and, directly ahead, a group of people had gathered on a rough stone jetty. Among them Eth recognised Hurli, and the resident dreamweaver in her dusty black gown.

Picking up her child, Arlynn went running towards them. "Meera! Hurli! Guess who's just arrived!" she cried. But Eth simply stood there and made no attempt to follow. She stared at the marsh, the reed-beds and osiers and stretches of open water, islands of willans and a few taller trees – screams of birds wheeling above it – the life of it, the sweet-rotten smell of it, the green–brown vastness going all the way to the horizon. And some way out the alien ship, like a gigantic metal beetle, was sunk to its belly in bog.

"Well, well," murmured Cable. "So this was Vashlian's intention."

Eth's heartbeat quickened with an upsurge of emotion. For seven long years, right from the beginning, Vashlian must have planned for this, used Eth herself and the Dreamweavers' Guild and anyone else he needed to make it happen. He had cared as much as she did about the fate of those people. Or had he? Maybe he, too, was ruled by the Dreamweavers' Guild and it was only Arbroth that concerned him, its peace and stability the aliens had threatened to destroy. Yet she knew Vashlian worked with the Guild only when it suited him, so he must have wanted the ship to land on Malroth for an altogether different reason.

He was a visionary, Cable had said, and dimly, vaguely, Eth began to understand the extent of his vision. There were three thousand people on board that ship, people from another world with a working knowledge of science and technology that was outlawed on Arbroth. And the cargo hold was crammed with machines that could help them survive. They could make Malroth habitable again by the same means Eth's own people had once used to ruin it. Next to her, Cable put down their bags.

"You'll get to meet Troy in the physical dimension after all," he said.

"Yes," said Eth.

"And will you still love him?"

"If I do," said Eth, "it won't become manifest."

"You can be certain of that?" asked Cable.

"Completely certain," Eth said firmly. "Whatever Troy and I are to each other doesn't belong in this dimension, Cable."

Cable smiled, reached for her hand, and they

stepped through the doorway together and walked towards the jetty. Eth could feel the wind in her hair, the sun on her face, the ochre red sands soft beneath her feet, a love for the place stirring inside her. Fragments of a fallen statue lay about – a cloven hoof, a weathered torso, a horned head with the evil eroded from its eyes – El-Tesh, the god her ancestors had once created, stripped of his power and no longer worshipped.

And did they bring their own gods with them? Eth wondered. Those alien people who sought to escape from their own despoiled planet? Did they bow still to a religion that elevated some above others, the bandit code of Liadd and Aldo that Vashlian sought to temper? Or had they left all that behind, as the people of Arbroth had done, willing to begin again and heal their auras as they healed a world? Eth did not know, but she could picture it in her mind: Malroth growing green again, the deserts beginning to bloom, exiles and aliens working together and learning to co-exist. It was a dream as yet – her dream and Vashlian's – but she was willing to share it, weave a vision into three thousand alien minds.

CHAPTER TWENTY-THREE

The ship had been forced down to land in the marsh,
stagnant water and reed beds all around it, a desert
shore almost a mile away. Automatically, on impact,
the cryogenics switched off. And now it was official.
Three thousand resuscitated passengers had been
informed of the situation, although the reason why
they had been diverted was not divulged honestly.
That a fault in the on-board navigational computer
had fouled up their original trajectory was all most
people knew.

"But what does it mean?" asked Mrs Guttenham.

"It means we've landed on the wrong planet!"
snapped Mr Guttenham.

Standing by one of the open hatches nearby,

watching the yellow inflatable life-rafts being loaded with supplies from the cargo hold, Troy turned his head as the Guttenham family approached. As a member of the crew it was his job to reassure them, or direct them for counselling if need be.

"Where are we then?" Mrs Guttenham asked plaintively.

"Don't you understand anything, Mum?" asked Ivan.

"We're on an adjacent planet in the same solar system," Hannah explained. "An awful place, by the look of it. All marsh and desert and virtually uninhabitable."

But not uninhabited, thought Troy. Even from their low vantage point, the ship's heat-seeking scanners had picked up several large unknown life-forms deep within the marsh, reptilian or amphibian probably, and possibly there were land animals that prowled round its margins. No one would know for sure until the advance parties returned from reconnoitring. But as far as Troy was concerned a landfall on this planet was not the end of the world. And nor was it the end of Eth's world either. Although he would never see her again and never get the chance to put things right between them, his relief outweighed his sadness. For the sake of the people on Arbroth he was thankful that the ship and everyone on board it had been turned away, the Guttenhams in particular.

"We won't have to stay here, will we?" Mrs Guttenham asked anxiously.

"For crying out loud!" Ivan said crossly. "How thick can you get? This ship wasn't constructed to take off again, Mum! We're stuck here! All of us! Whether we like it or not!"

Hannah pressed her nose against a porthole.

"We'll just have to make the best of it," she said matter-of-factly.

As would they all, thought Troy, because no amount of grumping and grousing could change the fact that they were there, three thousand people stranded on a barren planet. And having fouled up their own planet it was what they deserved, perhaps, a kind of poetic justice.

"But we can't possibly live on a world like this!" Mrs Guttenham said fearfully.

"We have no alternative," Hannah insisted.

"Someone is going to pay for this!" declared Mr Guttenham. "Heads are going to roll, believe you me!"

"So what are you going to do?" asked Ivan. "Lynch a couple of Flight Officers? And how will that help? Try facing it, Dad. We're in this together, everyone, crew and all, for the rest of our lives! We can't afford to start a civil war!"

Unlike his father, Ivan Guttenham spoke sense, Troy admitted grudgingly. And just as Troy himself had done with Bill and Verity, Ivan was willing to challenge his parents' view of things. He was also young enough to accept the situation, and change if he had to, in order to accommodate it. It was what they would all have to do, Troy supposed, change their thinking, change their ways and learn to work together.

Mrs Guttenham dabbed the tears from her eyes.

"However will we survive?" she whimpered.

"Easy," Ivan said brutally. "We'll all have to live crammed up in Portacabins, Mother. Muck in together. Reclaim land from the desert or the marsh in order to grow food…"

"I didn't leave my nice home and come all this way to live like that!" Mrs Guttenham objected tearfully. "And who's going to do all the hard work involved?"

"We are," said Hannah.

Mrs Guttenham gazed at her daughter in alarm. "Not us personally, surely?"

"Who else is there?" demanded Ivan.

"No one will expect you to take up manual labour at your age, my dear," Mr Guttenham said brusquely. "I'm sure we can depend on the ship's crew to do whatever's necessary, however incompetent they may have been."

Troy bristled, clenched his fists against the upsurge of anger, and along the corridor Ivan Guttenham glanced towards him. There was no liking in the youth's blue eyes but there was a kind of comprehension. Ivan recognised that beneath the silver uniform which marked Troy out as a member of the crew there was a human being no different from himself or any other passenger. Ivan turned to his father.

"We can hardly make slaves of our own kind!" Ivan said curtly. "We've done that too often in the past and it always leads to trouble. I think the time has come, Dad, for us to accept what we never did on Earth – that from now on everyone's equal and it's share and share alike, including the work."

"That's right," agreed Hannah.

Troy hesitated.

He had despised the Guttenham family from the moment he set eyes on them: their materialistic values and ambitions, their dreams of a palace and a million-acre spread. But now their dreams had turned to dust and the planet they had come to offered them little or nothing above what it offered him. Marsh and desert erased the differences between them. When they disembarked they would indeed be equal. And if Hannah and Ivan could acknowledge that, then so could he. Troy smiled briefly in their direction and was rewarded by a similarly brief nod from Ivan, and an answering smile from Hannah. She came towards him. Seven years sleeping had not aged her. She was still young and pretty, with wide blue eyes and long fair hair. And perhaps, when he told Eth he fancied her, he had not exactly lied.

"My name's Hannah," she informed him.

"I'm Troy," he told her.

"Have we met before somewhere?"

"Back at the space-station," said Troy.

"I'm not sure I remember," said Hannah.

"It was a long time ago," said Troy.

He moved to let her stand beside him in the open hatch. The sunlight made rainbows in her hair and just for a moment he wondered how Eth would have seen her, what colour her aura was and how badly contaminated. He pushed the thought aside. Eth had been a dream to him and she always would be, a girl from another dimension, another world where Troy had not qualified to land. And even if he met her face to face, what he felt for her was not translatable into physical terms.

But Hannah Guttenham was different. She belonged where he belonged, in a flesh-and-blood reality. With her he could begin again. He could love her as he already loved this world, although it was not Arbroth. It was alive, as the space-station had never been. The dry, dust-laden wind blew in his face, sighed through the reed beds and made a thrill inside him. Birds wheeled free above his head in a sky of cerulean blue, and even the reek of the quagmire smelled sweet. Below, the first inflatable life-raft headed along a channel of open water, and beyond it, past an island of trees, he could glimpse the shoreline, red desert dunes sweeping away to the horizon. The distances beckoned, and with Hannah he could dream a future there.

"Welcome to Malroth," said Troy.